RULES
for
STEALING
STARS

RULES
for
STEALING
STARS

COREY ANN HAYDU

 KATHERINE TEGEN BOOKS
An Imprint of HarperCollins Publishers

Katherine Tegen Books is an imprint of HarperCollins Publishers.

Rules for Stealing Stars
Copyright © 2015 by Corey Ann Haydu

Library of Congress Cataloging-in-Publication Data
Haydu, Corey Ann.
    Rules for stealing stars / Corey Ann Haydu. — First edition.
        pages   cm
    Summary: "Four sisters rely on each other—and a bit of mysterious magic—to cope
with their mother's illness"— Provided by publisher.
    ISBN 978-0-06-235271-2 (hardback)
    [1. Sisters—Fiction. 2. Magic—Fiction.   3. Family problems—Fiction.   4. Sick—
Fiction.   5. Mothers and daughters—Fiction.]   I. Title.
PZ7.H31389Rul   2015   2014047921
[Fic]—dc23   CIP
                                                                          AC

Typography by Carla Weise
15 16 17 18 19   CG/RRDH   10 9 8 7 6 5 4 3 2 1
❖
First Edition

To my very first friend, Dana,
and my very first librarian, Timmie:
for the love of stories, moments of magic,
changing New England seasons,
happiest memories

RULES
for
STEALING
STARS

one

Everything is standard Sunday morning today except for a streak of glitter on Astrid's cheek and the way never-tired Eleanor keeps yawning like a cat.

And of course, the house itself, the one Mom grew up in that we are now being forced to finish our growing up in: old and wallpapered in mostly pink and yellow roses and filled with photographs of Mom when she was eleven, like me, or twelve, like Marla, or fourteen, like the twins, Eleanor and Astrid.

Dad's in charge of Sunday breakfasts, so I get a heart-shaped pancake, and Marla gets a pancake shaped like a teddy bear, and Eleanor and Astrid share a pancake as big as the entire pan, which they call the Monster Pancake.

Last year Eleanor said we could all have regular-shaped pancakes now, but Dad made a big speech about whimsy and never being too old for it. Then we talked about the "Myth of Peter Pan" and staying youthful and playful forever or something. Dad's a professor specializing in fairy tales and stuff, so it was all pretty typical.

"How do you want your pancake, sweetie?" Dad says to Mom. We all heard her telling Dad she didn't want to get out of bed this morning. We all heard Dad coax her downstairs.

"Not hungry," Mom says. "Coffee fine." When she speaks in fragments instead of full sentences, it is a bad sign. When she won't participate in family rituals like Sunday morning pancake shapes and pajamas, and singing along with radio and TV jingles filtering in from the living room, it is a bad sign.

"I'll get the coffee!" Marla says. Her voice is overbright. She is smiling and eager. She's only ever this way around Mom. We are all different around Mom—exaggerated, desperate versions of ourselves. Astrid is spacier, Eleanor is sweatier, Marla is sweeter, and I am sillier. It's probably why everyone but Astrid calls me Silly. Not Prissy or CC or Cilla or any of the other 117 nicknames you could come up with for the name Priscilla. Just Silly. Always Silly.

Marla pours Mom a cup of coffee. It's a precise movement, like coloring in the lines or measuring a cup of flour. Nothing splashes onto her hand or the counter, and for a moment, Mom is enjoying her first sip of coffee and Marla is peacock-proud and Eleanor and Astrid are actually at the table instead of whispering secrets or squirreling away in their bedroom for hours without me.

For the one moment, I am not totally devastated we moved to the summer house in New Hampshire and away from our home in Massachusetts, and I think: *Yeah, okay, this feels good.*

I sing along with some local mattress store commercial playing in the background. Astrid hums and giggles; it's always been easy to make her laugh.

"What's on your cheek?" I say, since it's easier to ask questions when someone's laughing and happy and relaxed.

She reaches for the glitter on her face and with a swoop of her finger it's gone, like magic.

Astrid's eyes look paler and her skin rosier.

"Don't watch me so closely," she says. "It makes me nervous. Like you're going to figure us out." She winks and it's possible that she's making a joke, but it's every bit as possible that she's telling me she truly has something to hide.

They've been cagey lately, my big sisters. The twins keep disappearing into their room, which they always do when we're at the New Hampshire house. But now that we live here, it's even worse. I have asked a dozen times what the big deal with their room is and why they sometimes wedge a chair under the doorknob to lock me and Marla out when they're in there, but they only ever smile and tell me they'll take me to get candy later.

I don't want candy. I want to know what they're doing all the time, locked in their room. I want to be one of them.

"Another Monster Pancake?" Dad asks. He twirls his spatula like a baton and does a sort of jig along with our singing and humming. It's goofy and childish and embarrassing but mine.

"I think we're done, right?" Eleanor says, giving Astrid a look that isn't hard for anyone to decipher. She is declaring Sunday morning over, and special twin time beginning. I'm not ready to let the morning go, though.

"I'm not done," I say. "I'll have another pancake." Eleanor clears her throat and reaches for her phone, which has been going off with dings and buzzes and snippets of pop songs ever since the move six weeks ago. She says it's her friends back home calling her, but I'm almost sure that's a lie. LilyLee, my best friend from back home, doesn't call or text or chat nearly that much, and she's a pretty dedicated friend.

Besides, everyone knows Eleanor has a secret boyfriend, even if she won't admit it.

Everyone meaning me, Marla, and Astrid. It's not the kind of thing we tell Mom and Dad. That's what makes him a secret.

"Can we be excused?" Eleanor says. I'd like to clamp my hand over her mouth and superglue her to the chair.

"Come on," I say. "Can't you hang out for a few more minutes? Can't we do something together? I'm bored."

"Silly," Mom says. "Don't whine. You sound like Marla." It's not great that her only few words this morning are about me bothering her. She is wearing the same clothes as she was yesterday, and they are wrinkled and slept-in.

It's official: she is not doing well.

I don't look at Marla's face. It will be crumpled with sadness after that comment.

"Don't you get bored here?" I ask Mom. I mean it as a real question, not a whiny one, but I'm not sure she can tell the difference right now. Dad makes a dozen mini pancakes. Polka-Dot Pancakes, he calls them. They're the kind he likes best. He puts bacon in the pan too, but not for long. Like me, he likes his bacon soft and chewy. We have a lot in common.

"I get bored everywhere," Mom says with a shrug. Astrid

stares at her orange juice, and Eleanor wipes her own forehead. Marla pours Mom more coffee, like that is some sort of antidote for boredom.

"No one's bored," Dad says. "There's a lake. Go to the lake. You girls love the lake. Gretchen? You want to take them to the lake? I'll clean up here, pack you a picnic. You and the girls can spend some time together."

"No, thank you," Eleanor says before Mom has a chance to say no as well. "Astrid and I have a whole thing we're working on."

"I'll help," I say.

"It's not the kind of project you can help with," Eleanor says. Astrid looks sorry, like she'd like to say yes to me but can't. Eleanor thinks eleven is too young for everything, but Astrid knows eleven is not that young at all, especially in our family.

"I'm too tired to take anyone anywhere," Mom says. Of course she is tired. She was up all night doing her routine, where she wanders from closet to closet, opening and closing the doors. Sometimes she steps inside for a few minutes or an hour. She's always the saddest the mornings after her closet searching.

I stayed awake last night too, listening.

I opened the door to my own closet, trying to see whatever it was Mom was seeing. But all I saw were old suitcases and winter coats. I can't even step all the way inside my own closet, it's so full of things that smell like dust and grandparents. It seems like more things get piled in every year. Like someone is sneaking in extra coats and duffel bags and rain boots and broken umbrellas.

"We'll watch a movie later," Astrid says. "We'll play Monopoly. We'll make a collage to send to LilyLee." Astrid kisses my forehead, a thing that no one else ever does. That one gentle touch against my sunburned skin is enough.

I've stopped needing very much at all.

two

I knock on Astrid and Eleanor's door in the late afternoon when the house is lonely and quiet. No one answers. No music is playing. I don't hear their voices. I don't smell anything or sense any movement behind the wooden door with the hand-painted ELEANOR AND ASTRID'S ROOM sign on the front.

I am officially crazy curious.

Marla catches me with my ear against the twins' door. She sniffs, this noise she makes when she thinks she's better than me.

"They won't tell you what they're up to," Marla says.

"They won't tell you either," I say.

"They already did," Marla says.

I can't tell if she's lying. Marla is the kind of person who lies, but not if she's positive she could get caught. I squint, trying to see her better, but all I see is her dark mane, knotted at the ends, and her big blue eyes and the way her skirt rides up too far on one side.

Marla reaches for the doorknob, like she's about to go in, and I seethe with jealousy. It comes all fast and unexpected, a feeling with force.

"We have to protect you, remember? That's what Mom says. You're special or whatever," Marla says. She's always mad at me for things that aren't my fault, like the way Mom babies me even though she barely is able to even vaguely support or interact with anyone else a lot of the time.

Before I have a chance to respond, we hear a crash over by the stairway. Multiple clunks. A yelp. And a little-girl cry.

"Gretchen?" Dad, from his office, has heard the same series of noises. He doesn't call out to see if me and Marla and the twins are okay. I don't know if my sisters notice that kind of thing, but I always do. When a crash or a bang or a yelp happens in LilyLee's house, her parents call out to ask if she's okay. When it happens here, Dad rushes to Mom. He breezes past Marla and me in the hallway and peers down the stairs. We follow him and see her in a lump at the bottom.

"Oh!" Marla says, and rushes down before Dad is able to hold her back. Mom is crying the kind of tears that don't make noise, and she's hovering her hands over her ankle as if she'd like to hold it but can't bring herself to touch the tender part. We hover too, the three of us reaching toward, but never touching Mom.

"I fell," she says, and I'm laughing because it's such an obvious statement that it must be a joke, but Dad doesn't laugh, and Marla's breathing speeds up. I look at Mom's face to see if she was being dry and funny the way she sometimes is in upsetting situations, but she's glazed over and pale.

"What do we do? What do we do?" Marla says. She's waving her hands like she's trying to shake bugs off her fingers.

"Let's lift her up," Dad says. "Marla and Silly, can you help me get her to the couch?"

"Silly should go to her room," Mom says. Even now, even in her state of absentness, she's doing this weird protective thing. "This is probably a little scary for you, right, Silly?"

I shrug. I don't think I'm any more or less scared than Marla.

"I don't want you to see this," Mom says. "Go to your room." Like it's fine for Marla to see everything bruised and bloody and blurry and out of place.

"What about me?" Marla says. I would say she asks this

exact question at least a dozen times every week.

"We need your help!" Mom says. "Silly's too little for all this." Mom's words sound mushy and soft. They wind together, overlapping and turning a sentence or two into one mega-word.

"Right. Yeah. Of course," Marla says. She hooks her hands around the back of Mom's knees. She's moving like a cat, like a kitten, like the most delicate creature on earth. But Mom screams out in pain from the touch, and Marla scampers away.

"Okay, okay, let's call an ambulance, right? I have my phone here, so I'll do that? And we can let the girls go upstairs?" Dad puts a huge hand on Mom's head, a reminder of how very small she is in comparison. I wish he didn't say everything like a question.

"Stop trying to be Prince Charming," Mom says. Her voice has pins in it. Pins and knives and cactus needles and thorns. Everything sharp. She calls Dad Prince Charming a lot, and mostly with a sneer when Dad's trying to help her. It always catches him off guard.

Marla and I freeze, like sad marble statues, and I'm sure my breathing stops too, and my heart, and my mind. All of it freezes waiting for whatever's next.

"Go to your rooms," Dad says. "Both of you. Don't come out until dinnertime."

We don't go to our rooms. We go to Eleanor and Astrid's room.

Or Marla goes to their room, and I sneak in behind her. There's no chair under the door today, but they still don't want me to come inside. Marla tries to shove me out the door, but I hang on to the frame and stand my ground because I am a sister too, and she can't change that by being a completely impossible human.

"Oh. They're already gone," she says. Her shoulders droop, and mine do too, even though I don't know what we're missing, exactly.

Astrid and Eleanor are nowhere to be found, which is strange since I know they came up here earlier. But all over the floor and their beds and dressers are Astrid's shoe-box dioramas. She makes them all the time, but I had no idea she had this many. One for every day of the month. Maybe for every day of two months. I've never seen them all out at once, a collection of little scenes and imaginary worlds.

Pipe cleaners and glitter and construction paper and wallpaper samples and neon shoelaces and Christmas bows litter the room—the remnants of her creations. Astrid is the only person in the world who can make a brand-new universe with a few rhinestones, a bunch of wrapping paper, and Popsicle sticks.

Usually the dioramas are hidden under the bed or displayed on bedside tables.

"What is all this?" I ask, not really expecting an answer.

"It's for Eleanor's closet," Marla says. I have so many follow-up questions I'm worried I'll choke on them, but Marla drags me out of there and tells me to go to my room for the rest of the day or I'll never find out anything, and I either believe her or am so tired from all the commotion with Mom that I don't have the energy to argue.

They should call me Sleepy, instead of Silly, because that's mostly what I am these days. Sleepy and small, every time something else goes wrong in this terrible house.

three

The next day, I'm the only one awake in the whole house, even though it's past nine. Plus, I'm starving for pancakes. It's not Sunday, though, so there won't be any pancakes from Dad, and I don't know how to make them myself. Or bacon. I guess I don't know how to do much of anything. For instance, I'm freaked out by the iron, and no one taught me about doing laundry or fixing holes in my pants or talking to my mother. I can't do the useful things Eleanor is able to do or the sort of weird things Marla knows about—like folding hospital corners when she makes the beds or showing off her expertise with Mom's fancy label maker or deciding which attachment to use on the vacuum cleaner, based on what kind of surface you are vacuuming.

Dad comes down at ten. It's weird, since he's usually hard at work by now, either at the university preparing for classes, or working on one of his fairy-tale research projects. He made us sandwiches and brought them to our rooms last night for dinner, but he didn't let us come downstairs or see Mom when they got back from the hospital.

There are a lot of weird things about Dad, but one of them is that he doesn't really sleep. He doesn't seem to need it.

"Try not to worry," he says, instead of explaining anything that's happening.

Marla comes downstairs next. She's still pajamaed and slippered and shuffling her feet instead of picking them up to walk. Her too-long brown hair is in a not-quite-as-long brown ponytail, and her cheeks are blotchy. She picks up a cereal box to read the back of but doesn't start yelling at me for finishing off the Apple Cinnamon Cheerios.

She is different. Not a little. A lot.

"Where have you been?" I say. "What'd you guys do last night? And this morning?" After Mom's fall I sat in my room and read books and wrote LilyLee angry emails about how mean my sisters were being. I strategized ways to look and act older so they'll start treating me like I'm one of them.

Marla shrugs and smiles. She's beyond pleased that she's one of them now.

Eleanor comes downstairs next. She yawns the whole way down the stairs—from the top step to the sloping, broken one at the bottom. Her hair is a nest. It's hard to even recognize Eleanor when her hair isn't shiny and her clothes aren't pressed.

Then Astrid emerges. She is transformed too. Her blond hair is twisted and twirled on top of her head. She kisses my cheek and hugs Dad.

"Morning, family," she says, and just like that, because she's decreed it, we are a normal family for a delicate instant.

"It's late," I say. "We've been waiting for you." I nod toward Dad. He's wrapped up in a book with an old green cover and a bunch of Post-it notes.

"Silly. Let's be glass-half-full girls today. It's late morning, but it's not afternoon yet!" Astrid smiles, and I swear I haven't seen her smiling with actual teeth in months and months. It's not her style.

"That's nice," Dad says. He's smiling too, a real smile that goes to his eyes and even wrinkles his forehead a little. He heads to his favorite armchair on the porch, which is right off the kitchen, but if we are quiet enough, he won't hear us. I get a look at the spine of his book. *Sleeping Beauty*.

"Where were you yesterday? Did you go somewhere?

Were you hiding? Marla and I went to your room and you weren't there and Mom fell and—" I don't leave space in between my questions for answers, but Eleanor doesn't seem concerned about that anyway. She shakes her head. That's when I notice gold in her hair. At first I think it's summery blond streaks that we all get from the sun, but when I look more closely, it looks more like tinsel.

"Your hair . . ."

Eleanor tries to run her hand through it, but this morning her hair is knotted and half wet, and I know from the dampness of it and the way it glimmers that she has been somewhere. Again. She looks rained on, by both water and strands of gold, and she smells like pine trees and clouds, if clouds have a smell.

All my sisters giggle and I want to laugh with them, but it's too close to crying, and I think if I let anything out, it will *all* come out.

"We should make a perfect kitchen," Marla says. "Doll-house stove. Apple pie. Red checkered curtains." She's looking at Astrid, who nods like she knows what Marla's talking about, even though Marla is making no sense at all.

"This is a kitchen," I say. It is the world's lamest sentence.

"Don't worry about it," Marla says. "I wasn't talking to you."

"But I am worried about it," I say in such a small voice I think it is even less hearable than a whisper.

Mom hobbles into the kitchen. Her ankle's all wrapped, and she's in Dad's old robe. It doesn't fit her at all.

I'm sleepy again, on command. The sight of her makes me tired.

The opposite is true for Marla, who comes to life when Mom's around. She throws her arms around Mom's middle and heaves out a hefty "MORNING!"

"Not now," Mom says. She sort of flicks Marla away with her hand. Marla's face goes from happy to an angry frown.

"I'm going upstairs," Marla says to all of us and none of us. Eleanor and Astrid pop to attention and scamper after her.

"Can I come too?" I call after them. "Please?" The please is pathetic, and we all know it. Mom even winces on my behalf.

"Not right now," Astrid says. "Maybe later, okay?"

But Eleanor shakes her head like later is totally not going to happen.

"Give me a hint about what you're doing up there," I say. I won't follow them if they'll only tell me a tiny bit, let me in on even a small sip of the secret.

Astrid pauses on the stairs. She likes riddles and clues

and mystery. She thinks, all dreamy, her eyes rolled up to the ceiling.

"We're here, but not here," Astrid says. "We can go almost anywhere, but not move at all." She leaps up the rest of the stairs.

I get up and half follow her, but stop myself before I'm too pathetic. I'm stranded, standing near the bottom of the stairs.

I picture monsters and dragons. I picture black holes and haunted rooms. I picture fairies and princes and treasure chests. I picture all the things I've always been told aren't real, but must be.

Mom drags me back to reality, though. There is nothing more real and less magical than Mom's dark moods.

"Your sisters should be nicer to you. I should have included my sister more," Mom says, shaking her head at how quickly the girls ditched me.

"You don't have a sister," I say. Mom never talks about growing up, but I'm sure I would have heard about a sister if she'd had one.

"But I did," she says. Her eyes are red and confused. Even as she says the words, she looks like she doesn't believe them, and I know she's not totally in her right mind at the moment. Usually in the mornings she's pretty present, but not today.

"You did?" I say, one foot pointed in the direction of Astrid and Eleanor's room, and the other foot pointed toward Mom, wanting to understand what she's telling me.

"No. No, never mind," Mom says. "I don't want to talk about this now. I'm tired. I need some time alone, Silly." It's not the first time she's said something strange and wrong, but it was so specific and odd, the claim that she has a sister, I have to tell Astrid and Eleanor and Marla.

We need to be in this together. They can't leave me out here with Mom and her disconnected thoughts while they have some grand adventure.

Plus, I need to know what they're doing up there. What secret thing the twins have been up to the last few summers, and that Marla is all of a sudden allowed to do too.

four

Mom follows me upstairs. I thought she needed alone time, but sometimes Mom's moods change so fast it's hard to keep track, like she's playing some complicated kind of Ping-Pong with herself and I'm watching, trying to keep score.

She opens the hall closet, steps in for a moment like she's looking for towels or the vacuum cleaner, but comes out empty-handed.

"Mom? What's in there?" I say. I'm hovering outside the twins' room and would rather be in there, but not until Mom is tucked away in her bed for the rest of the day.

Mom runs her hands straight back through her hair. It

is fine and unwashed, so the strands stick and don't fall back into place. She sighs, a rickety sound that smells and sounds like cigarette smoke. She promised she would stop smoking.

"You think something's wrong with me!" she says. Her lips wobble. Her hands shake. She doesn't usually explode in my direction. I'm not important enough to explode at. "You think I'm a terrible mother. I don't understand why you hate the family so much."

"I didn't mean it," I say, but I'm stuck doing a strange math, the kind that is way too advanced for me. I don't have any idea how we got from me asking what she's doing to her being a terrible mother, but I'm squinting and counting on my fingers and speeding up my mind, trying to figure it out. "You're a great mom! I love the family. I wanted to hang out with the girls. I wanted to make sure you didn't need help with chores or anything. I didn't mean to be rude." I'm talking fast and loud and pretty much praying that my sisters will hear me and save me.

They don't.

"I've done the best I can," Mom says. She hangs her head and I imagine an enormous eraser, big enough to erase everything I've ever said that makes her feel this way.

"You're such a good mom," I say. "You're the best mom." I lean against the bedroom door and kick my heels against it a little, wish I'd learned Morse code when the boys in my class were all super into it two years ago. I could call for help through the pounding of my feet.

"So ungrateful," Mom says. Her mouth is turning down into its mean look, which I have seen from afar but never up close. These are the kinds of things Mom says to everyone, but never to me. This is the kind of conversation that always seems about to happen, but she'll ask Eleanor or Dad or Astrid to take me to my room before it spirals out of control. This is the first time Mom hasn't protected me from herself, and it hurts, makes me sick a little, but also reminds me of losing my first baby tooth or learning to read or getting on the bus for the first time. I'm joining my sisters. I'm growing up. They can't deny it anymore.

"I expected so much more from you," Mom goes on. "I'm so disappointed. Why do you think I'm like this? I never got what I wanted. You never give me what I want. You don't care about anything or anyone but yourself." She's talking to me, but also to a place on the wall next to me, her eyes shifting back and forth. I don't know if it's more terrible when she's looking right at me or when she's lost track of me and is speaking to the wall. "You're a terrible disappointment as a daughter."

I can't think of a way to escape, but Dad saves me before

it gets more desperate. He's on his way up the stairs.

"Gretchen!" he says, surprised at her words, I think, and maybe the swaying of her body. It looks like she's on a ship, not stable ground.

I get it. We're on rough waters.

"It's fine," Mom says with a slur, and I bet she doesn't even know what she's said, but I do and Dad does, and I have to wave my hand and shake my head and smile like it's totally okay and we're having some normal mother-daughter chat.

Mom starts yelling at Dad almost right away, and I should be relieved that he directed her away from me, but I don't want her to be yelling at anyone.

When the yelling reaches the highest volume imaginable, the door to the twins' bedroom finally cracks open, and a hand, Astrid's, pulls me inside. The yelling is only moderately quieter behind the door, but my sisters huddle around me, and when I nestle my head into their arms and shoulders and close my eyes, I can almost block it out.

"Are you okay?" Astrid whispers right into my ear, so that I can admit only to her if I'm not.

"Has that ever happened with you and Mom before?" Eleanor asks, but she knows it hasn't. She knows this is the day I have moved from special little Silly who needs protecting and turned into just another one of the girls.

It's weird, how something can feel good and bad at the same time.

"What'd you do to upset her?" Marla says.

"I hate this house," I say, which doesn't answer any of them, exactly, but also answers all of them, I think.

five

The curtains are drawn and the room is dark, except for a crack of light peeking through the bottom of Eleanor's closet. Astrid and Eleanor picked out heavy navy curtains when they decorated their new room, and they almost never leave them open, so it's night in here even when it's daytime everywhere else. Astrid says she works better with just a few night-lights on, and Eleanor is almost never inside anyway. So the way the closet light breaks through the darkness right now is unmistakable. A cut in the night.

I know instantly that's where their secrets are kept.

I guess closets are where we all keep our secrets. Dad

keeps the books that are too adult for us to read in his closet. Astrid and Eleanor have always kept pictures of boys they like in their closets. In my closet in our old house I had a story I wrote about me being LilyLee's sister and living with LilyLee's family. Of course now there's only other people's discards in my closet, which is yet another reason to hate the New Hampshire house. I don't even get a place to store my secrets.

Mom's secrets must be in closets too. Maybe she keeps extra bottles in there or something.

"I want to go in," I say, pointing to the line of light below their closet door.

"No!" Marla says, her voice cracking and desperate. A whole complicated series of looks are exchanged between the twins, and I understand that even if Marla was invited in before me, we'll always be the younger ones and they'll always have each other.

"She needs it too," Astrid says to Eleanor. "Don't you think?"

"I'm more than a whole year older," Marla says. It's not the first time she's used that as an argument for something. She's a stickler for a certain kind of fairness: if she wasn't allowed to swim to the deeper part of the lake until she turned eight, I shouldn't be allowed to do it until I turn eight a whole year later. Since she got a new bike when she turned ten, I shouldn't have one when I'm only nine. She wants her extra year on me to matter in some measurable way, whereas I'd rather pretend she and I are twins too, able to do everything together like Eleanor and Astrid.

"You can't leave me out there with Mom when you're all in here," I say, not realizing how true that is until I've said it. If there's a tornado, you all hold hands and anchor one another so that no one gets swept up alone. We are in the middle of a tornado, and it's not okay for them to hold on to one another and sacrifice me to the spinning, violent force. "It's not about how old I am. I can't do it all by myself. Didn't you hear how she talked to me? I can't be included in that but not included in this." I get a pang of fear that they won't listen. That I'll have Mom calling me a disappointment on the other side of their bedroom door while they all escape into secrets without me.

"I shouldn't be lonely when I have three sisters," I say, like feelings and families are simple scientific facts. Cause and effect.

There's a certain kind of shock on Eleanor's face, and I think she's never heard me say so many words at once, and so clearly.

"We're in charge, okay?" she says.

I nod. It's not anything new. They're always in charge.

Marla makes a series of noises that must be the

beginnings of words that she doesn't know quite how to finish.

Eleanor pulls the door to her closet open, and there's nothing inside but one of Astrid's dioramas. Not even a very good one. It's a basic park scene: aluminum-foil pond, green construction-paper grass, toothpicks with green pom-poms on top for trees. Orange Play-Doh dots that are meant to look like goldfish swimming in the reflective pond. Tissue-paper roses. It's pretty vanilla for Astrid, who usually likes her diorama trees pink and her diorama ponds covered in glitter.

"Do you like it?" Astrid says. I don't know if she means the diorama or the way they've positioned it in the middle of the closet. I shrug. "Like, is it a place you'd want to visit?"

"It's a park," I say, which isn't an answer. "It's a nice park," I amend, not wanting to say the wrong thing.

Astrid steps into the closet. Eleanor steps in beside her. Marla's next, and it's a pretty tight squeeze. I'm not sure there's room for one more.

I step inside and Eleanor closes the door. It goes dark and I close my eyes, a funny reflex I have when a room goes black.

Marla starts to giggle. Hearing Marla giggle is so new and strange I wonder if she's choking before realizing what the sound is. My eyes open because of the smell of roses. It's strong.

Overwhelming. I wonder if Eleanor's secret boyfriend has bought her some new perfume that she's spraying like crazy.

That's not it, though.

The ground is covered in green and yellow spikes of grass. At my feet there's a glassy pool of water. A small pond. I think I even see little orange fish swimming around right beneath the surface. I rub my eyes. There are roses everywhere, growing right out of the ground and not in bushes. We are in a very pretty park, the size of a baseball field.

I don't understand the things I'm seeing.

"We're in a park," I say. My feet won't move, and my sisters don't look confused enough, given what's happening.

"This is the best it's ever been, isn't it?" Astrid says to Marla and Eleanor. Eleanor nods and her eyes widen, but Marla shrugs, unconvinced.

"It's probably a good diorama," Marla says, her voice tight and fast, not leaving any room for other theories.

"Maybe all four of us together make the closet stronger," Astrid says. "We should have brought Priscilla in earlier." The sun's bouncing off the pond and her white-blond hair and the tips of our noses.

"Cautious is good," Eleanor says, but she's glowing in the sun too, and her jaw and elbows and shoulders look looser.

"What happened?" My voice screeches. They're all too calm. "How are we in a park? Is it . . . a time machine? Is this what you do? You go to parks? How do they— What do they—" I was so gung ho about having an adventure that I hadn't considered the way an adventure actually feels—prickly and terrifying. I want desperately to hold on to something steady, but nothing feels real or anchored here. "Help me understand."

"We bring in the dioramas," Marla says. I can tell she's trying to make it sound like she's done it a million times before, even though last night was the first time. "And they become real."

I start laughing, because it is a completely insane conversation that we're having.

"So Astrid's magical?" I say, thinking of the way her hands move so gracefully when she's making the dioramas. There's some magic there.

"The closets are," Marla says.

"*This* closet makes dioramas real," Eleanor says, "but Astrid's closet doesn't work." She crosses her arms over her chest. "This is the magic closet. The others aren't, okay?" She's speaking French basically. Or Japanese. Or pig Latin, which I know is supposedly really easy to understand, but I never am fast enough to keep up with.

"Enough with the talking! Look what I made for you!" Astrid says. She picks up a handful of grass and throws it at me. I'm surprised it smells real.

I finally take a step. The grass pokes the bottoms of my feet, and silky roses swipe my ankles. Immediately, I want it all. Not only the park and the smell of the outdoors and the way sunlight glints off the shiny pond. I want more. It's a funny impulse, given how much I now have at my fingertips. Like getting everything I want for Christmas but already making my Christmas list for next year.

I try to list every diorama Astrid's ever made in my head, or at least the ones I saw strewn all over their floor and furniture yesterday, but there are simply too many. Furry ones and sparkling ones and scary ones and perfect ones. She makes them, tweaks them, dismantles them for parts constantly, so it's an ever-changing collection of universes. Astrid's imagination is vast and strange and unexpected. And apparently, we now have a way to live inside it.

I'm goosebumping and blinking.

It smells like a park but also like a home. Birds, bright-blue ones, swoop in the sky and land on Eleanor's shoulders. They flap their wings against her face, and it seems to relax her.

"We let the closet take care of us," Astrid says. "And it always does."

We hold eye contact. In a lot of ways, Astrid's eyes are more surprising, more magical than anything in the closet. An almost neon blue, much brighter than even the birds, and never blinking.

I pick a rose. "You know these don't grow from the ground, right? Roses grow in bushes," I say. I don't know why this is the thing astounding me the most, but it is. Astrid shrugs. She's never been concerned with things like reality or facts or the world we live in.

The rose blossom moves in my hand. The petals open farther and farther, then it grows new petals to open even more.

"You're growing it," Astrid says.

"That. Is. Beautiful," Eleanor says.

"This isn't what usually happens?" I say. The rose grows. It's the size of my fist, then my head. It smells sweeter and silkier every moment.

"I knew it. We were meant to be in here all together," Astrid says. She has this serene look on her face, like everything's clicked, and Eleanor mirrors her soon enough. If one of the twins has a mood change, the other often follows. Twin domino effect.

Marla and I are in different universes, but the twins are living in the same square inch of land. I try to make eye contact with Marla, but she's staring at the center of the rose, and I'm left searching for something else to look at. This would never happen with the twins.

Eleanor leans over and touches the petals of the rose growing in my hand, and it expands even more.

With that, even Marla looks impressed. She sticks her nose into the center, soaking in the scent with a loud inhale. She's a different person in here. She can't stop laughing at the way the petals flop over, hitting her face as they grow.

Eleanor cracks up too and reaches into the pond for a lily pad. "Let's do this one!" she says, and we all touch it. In a moment, it grows to blanket size, big enough to wrap all four of us into a kind of sister-burrito.

Astrid's crying from laughing, and Eleanor keeps hugging me. It's so much better than anything I thought they might be doing up here.

We make all kinds of things grow and become more beautiful. We stick our feet in the pool of water and it sparkles. We hug a tree and it sways.

We do all of it together, since Astrid is sure that's the key to really accessing the full extent of the closet's magic. Togetherness. Sisterly-ness.

When we can't think of anything else to touch as a group, we do the most obvious thing. We play in the park. Like little girls and like sisters and like LilyLee's family, who always go on group adventures and spend afternoons together.

Marla settles on her back in the grass, which we made longer and greener, and Astrid spins around in circles until she gets so dizzy she falls over, then does it again. Eleanor sits by the pond and splashes the water, kicking her legs up and down so fast they're a blur, calling for us to join her.

I join Eleanor by the pond and dangle my toes in as well. Fish swim around my feet, tickling my ankles, and we are far, far away from our parents and the New Hampshire house.

"You've been keeping this from me," I say. If we were outside the closet, I think I'd say it meanly. I think I'd pout or something. But inside the closet, the sun on my shoulders and my ankles soaking in a pond filled with bathwater and gentle goldfish, I don't mind at all, I'm only curious what she'll say.

"We don't know if it's safe," Eleanor says. "We don't know anything."

"So?"

"Mom says we need to look out for you." A fish swims in between my toes.

Mom's always singling me out. "You're too smart for your own good, little one," she said only a few weeks ago.

"We have to keep you a kid, okay? Let's keep our Silly a kid." She was talking to all my sisters, and Eleanor and Astrid nodded and rolled their eyes, but Marla truly hated it. I think she wanted someone to care about keeping her a kid too.

Whatever that means.

"I guess she's not too concerned with protecting me anymore, huh?" I say. I can't quite grasp the image of Mom from a few minutes ago. I know I thought the look on her face would stay with me forever—stony but hazy. Unfocused but forceful. Right this moment, though, I can't pull up the image in my memory.

The goldfish slow and stroke my toes. A butterfly lands in my hair. It's an old, forgotten feeling, like when my mother used to scratch my head as I fell asleep.

Eleanor looks at me. Hard. It feels like she's trying to see if I've grown since the last time she looked at me.

She nods.

"We need this place," she says. And for the first time, when she says "we," it includes me.

six

The closet door is still there, at the edge of the park, when we're ready to leave. Waiting for us. Once it's open, the park fades before disappearing completely.

I think I might be sunburned. Mom and Dad are asleep or quiet or whatever it is they are after a drink and a fight and a lot of slamming doors.

I need to tell my sisters about the weird comment Mom made, about having had a sister, but I have too many questions about the closet first.

"So none of the other closets do anything at all?" I say.

Astrid and Eleanor exchange a look. Marla clears her throat.

"Mine doesn't do anything," Marla says.

Astrid is silent.

"The other closets don't work," Eleanor says. "I told you that."

Astrid stays silent.

"What about my closet?" I say.

"We can try it," Astrid says.

"Maybe someday," Eleanor says.

"It won't work either," Marla says.

"Who knows, now that we're all together, maybe everything will work," I say. "Like Astrid says." I'm sort of dreamy-feeling from the park. My brain feels like it's quilted or stuffed with down, pillowy and soft. Comfortable. I need it to last. I need my closet to work. I need to spend every afternoon in a new world in the closets, as strange and beautiful as today's park.

Astrid must be right, I think. It's what we get in exchange for a sick and sometimes mean mother. Sister-closet powers. It's what we get instead of a family that has dinner together every night with vegetable sides and cloth napkins and super-easy conversations about how everyone's day was.

"What kind of place are we going to visit next?" I say. My sisters all look tired. "LilyLee's family goes on vacations in the French Riviera. Can we make it look like the French

Riviera? I have a postcard, I can show you." The postcard I have isn't even that special. It's a curve of sand hitting a bright blue ocean, and white sailboats dotting the water. You can see the algae beneath the surface, a darker shade of blue. Pretty but not spectacular. I collect postcards, so I know which ones are truly beautiful and which are sort of blah.

I love the name, though. The French Riviera. It's a place where I could paint watercolors and drink drinks out of pineapples and eat little éclairs, which I know for sure are French.

"That's not how we do it," Marla says. She's already pissed, I can tell. Everything sweet from our time in the closet is fading fast. She hates that I'm a part of it now. She hates that we are better as a foursome than they were as a threesome. "Maybe you should leave the diorama ideas to Astrid."

"We can do so much better than France," Astrid says. Her hair's in her eyes, and she keeps having to pick it out. It's long and fine and gets whiter and whiter the deeper we go into summer.

"You coming with me tonight?" Eleanor says, abandoning the conversation like it doesn't matter at all, now that her secret boyfriend is obviously texting her.

"Where are we going?" I say. Eleanor laughs. Not

meanly, but enough that I know she still thinks of me as a lesser being. Our being a team in the closet doesn't matter out here, in the real world. She's drawing a line, with me and Marla still on the stupid-little-sister side.

"I was talking to Astrid. We're going out," Eleanor says, her voice taking on this haughty tone she uses when she's asking me to please clean up my stupid toys (even though I don't have toys anymore), or when she's explaining why eighth-grade math is way harder and more legitimate than fifth-grade math.

She starts trying on shoes. I had no idea she had dozens of sandals. Silver ones and ones with heels and ones with so many straps they look like torture devices.

"Where?" Marla says. I know when to give up, but Marla doesn't. She has a gloomy look on her face. It wouldn't be the worst idea to shove her back in the closet, I think. Have her stay in that peaceful state forever.

"Ice cream. Then a friend's house," Eleanor says. That means they're seeing her secret boyfriend. I say as much, and Eleanor huffs and won't reply, but she decides on these red flip-flops that Marla and I both covet.

"What about us?" Marla says. "You want us to take care of everything? Entertain Dad? Help Mom hobble around?" She's saying it like Eleanor and Astrid are leaving us forever, like we didn't just spend the afternoon together in their closet having basically the greatest experience ever. I wonder if Marla even knows how to be happy.

"We can go back in the closet together, Marla!" I say. "Astrid, can we borrow your planetary diorama? Will it work? Will we float around in space? Oh my God, I'm so excited."

"No!" Eleanor says. She turns red, redder than the sunburn from the park in the closet, redder than her red flip-flops, almost. "No closets without us. Absolutely not. Are you listening?" She's staring right at me, so she knows I am.

"Chill," Astrid says. She isn't trying on tops or shoes or hairstyles. I wouldn't be either. Eleanor is the only one of us who knows how to do those things. LilyLee's mother takes her clothes shopping and taught her how to French braid and how to match shoes with belts, and LilyLee says she taught her how to apply blush and eye shadow the other week too.

These are things we've never learned.

I'm pretty sure Eleanor's wearing too much blush, but I wouldn't know the right amount of blush, so I don't say anything.

"You went in without us," I say, hoping Marla will back me up. She doesn't, but she doesn't dispute me either. And with Marla, sometimes her not arguing with me is the same as her standing up for me.

"It wasn't some huge thing," Eleanor says. "We didn't do it that often until recently. Don't make a big deal out of it, Silly." Her cell phone is buzzing with texts from the secret boyfriend, and she's flitting her hands around nervously, but it doesn't stop her from being Big Sister Eleanor. "We're trying to keep you safe. No experimenting. New rule."

"There weren't any rules before you forced your way in," Marla says, like somehow this is all my fault now. Like without me holding her back, she'd have been able to go on closet adventures any time she wanted without any of Eleanor's wrath or Astrid's quiet worry.

"You look pretty," I say to Eleanor instead of agreeing with her or arguing with Marla.

"I do?" Eleanor looks genuinely confused. She stares at the mirror and combs her hair with her fingers. "There's this girl who works at the ice cream place, and she always looks perfect. Like her nails and the length of her dresses and a different necklace with every outfit. What's that like, do you think?"

"Boring," Astrid says. She throws a necklace around her neck. The kind with big plastic beads from the craft cabinet threaded with no pattern or sense onto a thick black string and tied with one of Mom's shaky-handed knots.

Sometimes I think I want to be more like Eleanor, who

tries so hard and is so pulled together. But right now I want to be Astrid, who doesn't care.

Eleanor and Astrid leave out the front door. The ice cream store is a short walk away, and Mom and Dad won't notice that they're gone.

"That'd be so cool," LilyLee said when I told her Mom and Dad don't notice, so we never have to ask permission to go anywhere or do anything.

LilyLee isn't always right.

seven

M arla and I try to have a nice evening alone together. Or, I try. Marla mopes.

We sit on the couch in the living room and watch TV, but after a while we're not watching TV at all. We're waiting for Mom to go back to bed. She is eating dinner by herself in the dining room and keeps dropping her utensils and swearing at them. She's drinking from a mug instead of a glass, which is a bad sign. It means she doesn't want us to see what's inside.

We're watching an old movie version of *Annie* that Mom turned on before she started dinner. I think we'd both like to change the channel—movie musicals aren't our thing—but sometimes when Mom is in a mood, anything can set her off. So we sit tight and tense on the couch and wince whenever a knife or fork clangs to the floor.

"I have something to tell you," I whisper. I think maybe Marla and I can figure out what's going on with Mom together, if I tell her about Mom's mystery-sister. Since Eleanor and Astrid want to leave us alone, Marla and I can have our own secrets. "It's about Mom."

"Mom's fine," Marla says, before I can tell her what Mom said.

Fine. I'll figure it out myself.

I sing along with *Annie* under my breath.

As expected, Mom doesn't ask where Eleanor and Astrid are, and Dad doesn't come out of his study.

Near the end of the movie, Annie sings the song "Maybe" for the second time. It doesn't do much for me, but I hear a sob coming from the other room. Mom.

If there is a worse sound than Mom crying, I haven't heard it. Everyone says nails on a chalkboard are the worst, but I'd take that any day over this.

Marla and I look at each other and reach for the remote, but when I get my hands on it, I can't decide whether to turn the TV off or lower the volume or do nothing at all.

"Should I get Dad?" I whisper, and slide closer to Marla on the couch. At least I'm not alone.

"He won't know what to do," Marla says.

"I don't know what to do," I say.

"Well, he'll make it worse."

Annie stops singing, but Mom doesn't stop crying.

"My sister loved this song," Mom says. I think that's what she says. Her words are mushy and slurred. I'm scared when she sounds like this. I want to shake her until the words come out clearer, crisper. I want to disappear, and I know exactly how to do it. I'm about to suggest to Marla that we sneak back into Eleanor's closet, that our sisters would understand if they knew how dire the circumstance was, but she gets up from the couch, puts her shoulders back, and clears her throat.

"I'll check on her," Marla says. It's a terrible idea. Night crickets chirp out warnings. The sun goes down the whole way. It's a sure sign, all of it, that it's too late to save anyone.

"Maybe you shouldn't do that?" I say. Eleanor would grab her elbow and jerk her back down to the couch. Astrid would distract her with an art project and a few bits of gossip about Eleanor's secret boyfriend. But I make a sound like a lamb and blink my eyes a lot and give up before the words are even out of my mouth.

"She probably wants company," Marla says. "She's probably lonely." I wonder if we're whispering low enough for

Mom to ignore us. The house seems too drafty and quiet, and the loud *Annie* finale hasn't started yet.

I should stop Marla, but I don't know how. I let her go. I run upstairs before I have to hear what happens to her. I don't want to know.

I'm a bad sister.

~ꬽ~

In my room I can't hear much of what's happening in the rest of the house. Sometimes I hate that, feeling disconnected from my sisters. Marla can hear the twins through their shared wall, and of course the twins have each other, even though Mom and Dad offered to let them have separate rooms in the New Hampshire house. I think they could tell Mom wasn't thrilled with the idea of turning her sewing room into a bedroom.

She doesn't like us going in the sewing room at all.

I try to distract myself by writing a postcard to LilyLee. The challenge of postcard writing is that you want to get across the most important things that have happened in the last few days, but you can't say anything too personal. It's an art form, like Astrid's dioramas, or at least that's what I tell myself.

I have a huge collection of postcards, and I go through five different pine tree New Hampshire ones, trying to craft the perfect three sentences to explain what happened today.

But I never get it right, because I can't stop looking at my closet door.

It looks like Eleanor's. The same white wood. The same blurry brass doorknob that could use a good shining. The same squeak of the hinges when I open it, which I do, slowly, like its magic might pour out if I'm not careful.

I'm going to go inside.

It's probably not magic, anyway. It's probably a normal closet like Marla's and Astrid's. Probably only Eleanor got the special closet, because Eleanor is exactly the kind of girl who would get a special closet. I am not that kind of girl. I don't deserve it.

I take all the clothes and shoes and broken umbrellas and suitcases and missing-strapped backpacks out of my closet. I am close to certain that Astrid and Eleanor unloaded their closets' contents into mine. Eleanor's closet is now empty of everything but magic. So I have to make a huge pile of other people's stuff in the middle of the room.

I consider getting one of Astrid's dioramas, since that's what makes the magic happen as far as I can tell, but I need to try to do this secretly, without getting in trouble. I don't want them to find out and keep me out of Eleanor's closet for good. And they'll notice a missing diorama. They might even notice a moved diorama.

When my closet's cleared of every last mitten and empty jewelry box and fleece vest, I walk all the way inside and close the door behind me. Wait with the light on for something to happen. Wait for nothing to happen. Wait.

The light is different than it looks from outside the closet. Warmer. More orange. Like fireplace light or candlelight or the light that comes from a perfect New Hampshire sunset that you watch from the woods, through the trees, out camping with Mom and Dad when Mom and Dad used to take us on camping trips during summers when Mom was doing well.

Then I see that the glass ceiling fixture looks all wrong. It's clear and delicate-looking, like a bubble about to be popped. It does not look anymore like something that has been screwed into the ceiling and has gathered dust for months. And the lightbulb inside doesn't look like a lightbulb anymore. It looks like the sun. A fiery one. A little terrifying, like it could fall from where it's floating above my head and crash into flames around me.

It's levitating and glowing and sort of bouncing from corner to corner in a slow, deliberate dance. Magic.

No diorama necessary, I guess. I thought I wouldn't be able to do anything in here without a diorama and without the rest of my sisters, but if anything, it's even stranger and sparklier than Eleanor's closet. It's not an imitation of a place in the real world. It's a brand-new thing, something I've never seen before. I knew orange and pink and gold existed, and I guess I'd seen them bleed into each other in certain sunsets, but never like this.

This is a new color. And a new quality of light. A new series of movements.

I close my eyes, like maybe the vision has something to do with my tiredness or the fact that I have glasses I got and broke and never really wore. But when I open them again, the lightbulb is even rounder, pinker, oranger. *It's happening,* I think.

I throw the door open. It's not that I don't want to spend hours looking at the transformed, moving light. I do. But I also want the world to make sense, and with the door open, it does again.

With the door open, the light is a lightbulb. The fixture is dirty ceramic, a gray that used to be white. The closet is once again a closet with dust bunnies and water damage on the walls.

My closet is magic too, I think, over and over on a loop. *My closet is even more magical,* I think after another minute. I don't need dioramas. I have something else. I don't know what, but it's something all mine.

Or maybe I only have a magical lightbulb. Who knows? Even that would be enough.

I'm thrilled and terrified at the same time, and I didn't know how wonderful these two things could feel when mixed together. It's like the first time I ate peanut butter and honey, or when Eleanor made me an apple and cheese and mustard sandwich.

I step all the way out of the closet and slam the door shut. My legs won't stop twitching, even though I take deep breaths. I bend my knees, doing weird aerobics the way Mom used to do in the living room sometimes when it was blizzarding outside and she couldn't go for a run.

Mom hasn't gone for a run in a long time.

"Eleanor?" I call out. She and Astrid should be home by now. It must be pretty late, and they wouldn't stay away all night, I don't think. They wouldn't do a sleepover without asking permission, even though they could get away with it. But she doesn't answer. "Astrid?" I try. I'm not even sure how loud I'm calling. It could be a whisper, for all I know. I'm too overwhelmed to really assess anything. But Astrid doesn't answer either. I mean, she barely hears me when we're in the same room and I'm making eye contact with her, let alone when we're in different rooms doing entirely different things.

"Marla . . . ," I say. This time I know it's a whisper. I'm not sure I actually want Marla to come running, but I'm sort of out of options, and at least if she were here, I wouldn't be alone with whatever it is that's happening. "Marla!" I call, louder this time.

And of course it's Marla who appears, pushing my door open when she hears her name. Her eyes are rimmed in pink. It's from crying, although there was a period of time a few months ago where Eleanor was sporting that look on purpose. Someone told her pink eye shadow was in. She didn't believe us when we said it looked weird.

Same went for the black eye shadow phase, when it constantly looked like she had been punched in the face.

"We do our best to learn stuff without Mom, you know?" Astrid said when I was making fun of Eleanor. It shut me right up, that's for sure. I almost tell Marla that I'm thinking about all this right now, but it's not the right thing to say, and I know it. She's sad and I'm freaked out and exhilarated, and our sisters will be home any minute, so I need to get out what's happened now so that I can fight the impulse to tell Eleanor and Astrid that I broke the rules.

"I did it," I say. I can't put words to the specifics, so I take her hand and try to pull her into the closet.

"Stop! What are you doing? Don't grab at me!" Marla has a hitch in her voice, confirming the crying she's been doing since I left her with Mom. Between Marla and Mom, we could fill all of Blue Lake with tears.

Of course the lake down the street is called Blue Lake.

As Astrid's always saying, most people in the world have a serious lack of imagination, and I guess New Hampshire is no exception.

Meanwhile, I haven't cried at all. I couldn't fill a thimble, let alone a whole lake. I considered doing it when we moved, but decided I didn't really need to.

"Are you okay?" Marla says. I'm not sure Marla's ever asked me that. She's usually very worried about her own big huge feelings, and not so much concerned about anyone else's. A little bit of me warms up inside, seeing her eyebrows all scrunched together.

"Something happened in my closet," I say.

"No," Marla says with some force, as if she could change what's already happened by saying *No* with enough feeling behind it. "You're not anything special. Your closet's not anything special. I don't know what you think you saw, but it probably wasn't real, and you should probably forget all about it." Even Marla knows how flat her argument sounds. In the pause after her words, I reach out a hand and put it on her shoulder, the way Eleanor might. Marla leaps away from me.

She doesn't leave my room, though, doesn't cover her ears with her hands and scream at me to shut up, which she has definitely done before, so I think I'm allowed to keep going, even if it stings a little.

I'm trying to work out the feelings, inside and out, and I need to say them to one of my sisters. "It was warm and strange. It was better than what's out here."

Marla doesn't reply, but her eyes go wide and glassy, and I wonder if maybe she's about to have another sobbing situation right here and now. Her fists are tight at her sides and I should stop talking, even if she isn't telling me to.

Maybe I'm a very selfish person or am so stunned that my mouth won't listen to my brain, but I keep going. It's like I shook up a can of soda and opened it, and now that the words and feelings and complications are fizzing out, it's not like I can twist the top back on to make it stop. It's too late.

"It was weird," I say. "Like a dream or a nightmare. But not scary, except sort of scary, because it was in my closet and I didn't know what was happening, and it would have been pretty if I was, like, outside watching the sky? Or if I had made it come to life from a diorama, but I don't know what might happen in there. It has a mind of its own. Eleanor's seems all comfortable and safe. Mine's different. It's impulsive or something. It's in control."

"It's so *unfair*," Marla says before throwing her hands in the air and stalking out of my room. I don't call after her; I wouldn't know what to say.

I'm on my own again, which is exactly what I was trying

to avoid. But the shakes in my leg have stopped, and a tiny bit of that warm-sun-lightbulb seems to be inside me now. In my veins, sort of. Or my heart. I guess I'm not sure. It's the beginning of a feeling and not a whole, complete, expressible thing yet.

It's almost nice enough to make me want to venture back into the closet, close the door again, stare at that lightbulb that maybe-possibly isn't a lightbulb, and see what else I can get. It feels like I swallowed a bit of the warm light. Apparently I needed that. I've been cold inside since Mom got sick again. This ugly moment in time comes with its own weather pattern. It comes with a chilly temperature down to my bones and a tightness in my chest and a funny dry taste in my mouth, like I'm craving a gulp of water.

So the warmth in the closet, the orange light, the hypnotic dance it did above my head, felt especially good. I want more.

But not alone.

eight

It used to be that we would all sleep through the night. It used to be that once my lights were off and my door was closed, I would be all alone until the next morning.

I guess it's not that way anymore.

Sometime after midnight I wake up and Astrid is sitting at the foot of my bed, and Eleanor is hovering above me.

"What did I tell you?" Eleanor says. I am waking up from a dream about frogs and princesses, so it takes me a while to figure out what she means.

"Mmmmm," I say.

"I said not to go in any closets while we were gone," Eleanor says. Astrid doesn't say anything. She does, however, keep a warm hand on my foot, which has snuck out from under the covers. I decide it's her way of telling me she's not as mad at me as Eleanor is, or maybe even that Eleanor isn't as mad at me as she seems to be.

"You left. You wanted ice cream," I say. It's not an accusation, it's the truth.

"What does that have to do with anything?" Eleanor says. "Marla woke up with nightmares because you went in there alone. She almost went and got Mom. Not okay! Didn't you listen to Astrid? Didn't you hear her say that we are maybe all supposed to be in there together? Why'd you have to go and ruin that?"

"I didn't ruin anything! I just gave it a try, to see if mine was special too. So we wouldn't miss out. We can all go in it now!" I say. Maybe I am better at standing up to my sisters when I'm half awake and partly dreaming, because my voice is clearer and stronger than ever before.

"We trusted you, and you went ahead and did this anyway. We should never have let you in to begin with," Eleanor says. A small part of me believes her, that I was being bad when I tried out my own closet without them, but then I remember all the summers that they've been going into their closet without me. And the last few weeks when they've left me alone in the drafty kitchen at breakfast, wondering if Mom has coffee or wine in her mug.

Even the way they disappeared to get ice cream was wrong. If they didn't want me to go in alone, they shouldn't have left me alone. That's what I'm thinking, even if those aren't the exact words that get out.

"It's my closet," I say. "Marla shouldn't have told you, anyway. She had no right to tell you. I thought she was on my team." Eleanor shakes her head like I don't understand anything at all, and Astrid squeezes my foot, which either means *it's okay* or *stop talking.* I stop talking.

"We're all on the same team. We're on team Don't Get Hurt in Some Scary, Unknown Closet That We Know Nothing About," Eleanor says. "It could be like mine, or it could be something all its own." She is speaking too loudly for midnight. Astrid tries to shush her, but Astrid is not really the shushing type, so it comes out less like a shush and more like a sigh. "The closets aren't all good, you know," Eleanor goes on. Her eyes are slits, and she has the same look on her face she used when we told scary stories last summer using flashlights and whisper voices.

"Don't freak her out," Astrid says in her very quietest voice.

"There have to be rules! Her closet might be bad like yours!" Eleanor practically yells. I shush her too. My shush comes out more like a regular shush, but Eleanor doesn't like it, and she wrinkles her nose in my direction.

"Whose closet is bad?" I say. They said the other closets didn't work, not that the other closets were something to be really, truly scared of.

"You think we're telling you more secrets now?" Eleanor says. She's too close to shouting, and if she doesn't quiet down, Mom or Dad might wake up. "We're wishing we could un-tell you secrets. We're not about to tell you or Marla more now."

"You said Marla and I aren't a team anyway," I say. But I always knew we were, and I feel a little bit glad to not be the only one on the outside.

"Enough with the teams." Eleanor rolls her eyes, because the twins have never understood why Marla and I would be jealous of their automatic allegiance. Eleanor and Astrid take it for granted, how special they are together, how bonded they are, how full and bright and shiny their private world together seems.

In some ways, Eleanor and Astrid's twinship is its own magic closet, filled with mysterious things no one else can see or experience.

"Show me what happened in there," Eleanor says. I'm not able to argue with her serious tone, and I think maybe if I tell her all about it, she'll be excited with me instead of disappointed and angry. So I start describing the lightbulb and the orange glow.

The warmth.

"No," Eleanor says, walking to the closet and opening the door with a flourish. "Show me." She steps into the closet, turns on the light, and crosses her arms over her chest. She's sweating. I wonder if it's because she's nervous about the closet or if she had a Mom encounter when she came back from seeing her secret boyfriend. Most of Eleanor's sweating is Mom-related. Astrid and I follow her, and I shut the door behind me.

"What did you bring in with you earlier?" Astrid says.

"I didn't bring anything," I say. Eleanor looks at me funny. Astrid coughs.

We wait for the closet to do its thing, and soon enough the light turns a pinkish color and the orb spins and lowers and the whole thing is much more frenetic and hyper than the lovely, slow dance from earlier. The light flickers a speedy rhythm, like a strobe light; then the spinning hastens and the orb that used to be a lightbulb shrinks to the size of a dragonfly, grows wings, and buzzes around the room, goading us on. Eleanor presses herself against the wall and looks like she wants to leave, but I chase the bug that used to be a light. It's like trying to swat a mosquito when it's buzzing in your ears, but instead of waving my arms around to scare it into leaving, I'm waving my arms around trying to outrace it and get it cupped in my palms.

"I don't like this!" Eleanor says. "This isn't relaxing! This isn't why we do this!"

Astrid sits with her back against the wall and giggles, watching me. I think this is exactly why we do this. My heart's pounding in the good way, the way that lets you know you're alive and capable of having fun.

"Look at Priscilla. Stop thinking about yourself. Look," Astrid says to her twin. I am getting out of breath, racing back and forth. The closet expands to accommodate my burst of energy and my desire to play tag with this *thing*. At first it's only a few steps wide, then large enough to fit all the happiness I feel and the frantic energy of the buzzing orb. Larger than the whole house, it seems. I can't ever get the little thing in my hands.

"It's crazy enough out there," Eleanor says, gesturing to the closet door. "Why would you want more craziness in here?" I'm not sure if she's asking me or Astrid, so I say nothing and continue running and waving and letting my heart buzz in time with the orb's little wings.

I can't believe we're letting Marla sleep through this. We are terrible sisters.

But she's a terrible sister too, for telling them I went inside without permission. So I guess none of us really know how to be good at the sister thing, which is weird, since we've been doing it our whole lives.

"This closet is Priscilla's," Astrid says. She looks so pleased, so ridiculously glad that I am having fun. I stop for a moment to catch my breath, and the orb keeps zipping around me. I liked Eleanor's closet, but Astrid's right, this one is distinctly mine in a very different way. Not homey and sweet, but buzzy and fun and thrilling.

Eleanor's eyebrows look like they are working very hard to reach each other across the bridge of her nose. I get the feeling there are still more and more secrets they are keeping from me, but it's hard to care when the orb buzzes near my ear and then dashes to the far corner. I sprint after it and laugh when it takes a sharp turn, changing directions and tripping me up.

"Don't you want to have fun?" I call out, but Eleanor leans against the wall and crosses her arms as I flop on top of Astrid in a giggling fit. Astrid tickles me, and for a moment we are younger and sweeter and sillier than we've ever been. I think if we were brothers we would play like this all the time: raucous and physical and piled on top of one another. But my sisters and I usually stay in our own spaces, touching for brief moments, then releasing.

I try to pull Eleanor into our wrestling, so that we can be a mess of limbs and laughter on the ground. I wouldn't mind watching the orb from down here—letting it do a dance above our heads. Swatting at it from our backs.

"Don't be scared," I say. It's the oldest I've ever been. But Eleanor shakes her head.

"You haven't seen what I've seen," she says. "You don't know about the bad closet." I can't stop myself from shivering, even in here.

"My closet—," Astrid starts.

"Not now," Eleanor interrupts.

Can't anything be just wonderful and nothing else?

"It's time to go to bed," Eleanor says. "We'll discuss the closets, all of them, in the morning."

I don't necessarily want to leave the warm, pink-lit space, but I'm too tired to put up a real fight.

The orb lands on my shoulder, and I wonder, for a moment, what would happen if I took it out with me. If it would fill my whole bedroom with its pulsing glow. I have a feeling that even though the diorama went back to normal when the door was open, this might be different.

I might be different.

I can't do it now. I'm certain Eleanor has all kinds of rules about that, too. But I don't have whatever creeping feeling she does about the magic. I have the sense that it would be okay if I took things out of the closet and into my world. Maybe Eleanor simply doesn't understand the closets the way I do. Maybe that's why her closet needs a diorama and mine doesn't. I let myself smile for three seconds, with the delicious idea that I know more than Eleanor for once.

～e⁓

We open the door and watch the magic fade.

"No more secrets," Eleanor says.

I blush, like she's heard what's inside my head.

And I'm so used to doing whatever Eleanor tells me to do, I almost share with them what Mom said, about the maybe-sister. Almost, almost, almost. These days it's my favorite word.

I almost tell them everything, but they look so sleepy and I feel so excellent and the opposite of anxious—UnWorried—that I decide it can wait.

nine

The next morning Mom's got her mug of hopefully-coffee and a plate with three slices of burnt toast. She likes it black. The kind of toast that makes the whole house smell like it's burning down.

"Have breakfast with your mom?" she says. Her voice is sweet so I can officially confirm she is drinking coffee, not wine.

"Sure. I'll make my own toast, though." Mom's burnt toast is one of those family jokes that never dies. It probably should have stopped being funny years ago, but we've kept it going, and it always gets at least a small smile from Mom.

"I can make you something. You want eggs? French

toast? I haven't made French toast in ages." I notice she's not in her bathrobe or her ratty, worn-through jeans. She's in a khaki skirt and this yellow shirt that isn't quite dressy but isn't sad and tired either.

"Yeah, French toast," I say. She makes it with cinnamon and hums to herself while moving the egg-soaked bread from a bowl to the pan. It's all going really well, until the fried cinnamon scent turns and the French toast starts to burn in the pan.

"What did I do?" she says. Her hands are shaking. I hadn't noticed until she picked up the spatula. I try to imagine myself back in the warm light of my closet. I wonder what would happen if I brought eggs in there. Would they hatch? Would something spectacular emerge? There's a pack of Post-its on the counter, and I grab one and scribble out the word *eggs* as a reminder. It looks like the start of a grocery list, but it will turn into a list of things to try in my closet.

"That's okay, it still looks good!" I say. "I'll eat it. It's all about the syrup anyway, right?" My cheeks hurt from how hard I'm smiling, and everything inside me has the same kind of ache—tired and trying too hard.

"I used to be so good at this," Mom says. She's not crying, exactly. She's flushed and embarrassed, I think, and it's actually much worse. I know what to do with the crying.

I don't know what to do about this. Her hands won't stop shaking. I hate it.

"You're a great cook!" I say, although Mom hasn't cooked since long before we moved to the New Hampshire house. The correct statement would be: When you're not sick, you're a great cook.

"Forget it," Mom says. The spatula is loose in her hands now, like she's given up so completely that she is fine with dropping it on the floor, mid-sizzle. The egg batter on the pan makes a sputtering noise, and the smell of burning egg mixes with the fried cinnamon scent. Mom puts the spatula on the counter with a sigh and turns off the burner.

"You don't have to eat it," she says, shrugging before leaving the room. I wonder, the moment she's gone, whether she was ever there at all.

I take a few bites of the French toast, but the taste makes me sad.

The house is quiet and Mom has floated back to her room, but Dad must be somewhere, so I look in all his usual hiding spots: the couch in the living room where he watches TV, the reading alcove upstairs with a book on myths and fairy tales and the yellow legal pad he takes notes on when he's in professor mode, the front yard with the tiny vegetable garden he's trying to grow, the back porch where he escapes with his paper.

Bingo.

"Silly!" he says, looking up at the sound of my hippo-slippered feet.

"Dad!" I say, imitating his tone and smile. It makes him laugh—a hearty, full sound that I love.

"How are you doing, princess?"

"I'm okay."

"Early morning for you, huh?" He folds his paper up, which means we are going to have a real talk. It rustles and flops in his face, and although at first he tries to make it neat, he gives up quickly and puts the whole messy thing aside.

"Couldn't sleep," I say. He nods seriously and puts his feet up.

"Still getting used to the new house?"

"Yeah," I say. "It's big. And old. And . . . there are a lot of closets." I don't mean to bring up the closets and hate that my sisters are right to worry about me telling Dad all our secrets. I know not to tell him the details, but I want his thoughts, I want his advice, even if I can't tell him what's actually going on.

"Scared of monsters in the closets?" he says. He's joking, but there's a gentle look on his face that I think means he won't tease me if that's what it is.

"I didn't have a closet in our old house," I say. Our

Massachusetts house didn't have many closets at all. Mom said she liked that about it. She liked buying wardrobes and dressers. Antique ones with delicate knobs and engraved wood.

Which is especially funny considering how obsessed she is with wandering into the closets here in the New Hampshire house.

Dad nods again, his same thoughtful, serious face, and lets out a long, rumbling *hmmmm*.

"You know 'The Twelve Dancing Princesses'?" he says after a moment.

"Isn't it some fairy tale?" I say. I take a seat in the rocking chair. It squeaks with every rock.

When Dad talks about fairy tales, especially princes and princesses, he gets this look on his face that reminds me of the look LilyLee's parents get on their faces when they talk about things like their wedding or their first date or what they did when they were our age. He's going to go off on one of his lectures.

"A princess fairy tale. A good one. Don't tell your mom, she'd be mad," Dad says. It's true. Mom won't read any books with princesses, won't buy us princess toys, or let us be princesses for Halloween. It's funny, considering how much Dad loves fairy tales, that he ended up with someone who hates them. A lot of things about Mom and Dad are funny, I guess.

"I don't tell her anything," I say. It slips out, accidental and huge. Dad pretends not to notice.

"These princesses, in the story, are exhausted every morning, so the king surmises that they must be doing something scandalous every evening. Oh, and they have shoes. Their shoes are all ripped up and worn out every morning. They keep needing new shoes."

Dad is actually terrible at telling stories. His voice is nice and he sounds all excited, and you can tell he really, really wants you to enjoy yourself, but in terms of actually making sense, he fails every time. I wonder if he's this way when he's teaching classes too, or if he's only bad at telling stories to his daughters.

"So he takes their shoes and gives them to this prince, and tells the prince to, I guess, find out what's wrong with the shoes? So the prince follows the girls into their closet, and inside is this magical world where they dance with other princes, or maybe not even princes, just really handsome boys, and the prince tells the king that's what the girls are doing every night. Dancing in this magical world they get to through the closet."

"Then he marries one of them?" I say. I don't mind the

story, actually. Even the way Dad's telling it. I like the big group of sisters, and I like their secret magical world, but I hate that in the end all that really happens is a wedding. That's how fairy tales always are.

"Then he marries one of them. He gets to choose which one to marry, since he solved the mystery."

"And the girls stop going dancing?" I rock more quickly. I like talking about the closets with Dad, even if he doesn't know that's what we're doing.

"I don't remember," he says. "I'll look it up and get back to you." Dad has these big books of stories from different cultures. Sometimes the same story shows up five different ways, told with a slightly different focus depending on the time and place and storyteller. I like that the same story can end so many different ways.

Eleanor and Astrid and Marla come downstairs a few minutes later and join us on the porch. Eleanor wrinkles her nose at the smell still haunting the air of French toast gone wrong.

They each have a piece of fruit and a bowl of cereal, and none of them asks what happened in the kitchen earlier. They know the answer.

"The Dancing Princesses have emerged," Dad says, winking in my direction.

"Mom hates princesses," Marla says, showing off for Mom even now, even when Mom is sleeping or doing whatever she's doing upstairs.

Dad picks his paper up again, the rustling of the pages signifying the end of the conversation, and we sit on the porch in silence, the mention of Mom heavy and hard enough to quiet us all.

ten

I'm going to sneak an egg up to my room. It won't be hard to do. I'm practically invisible right now. Dad's going for a post-paper run. Eleanor is texting her secret boyfriend, and when she's doing that, she doesn't notice anything else. Marla's baking something, and Astrid's working on a diorama at the kitchen counter, filling a black shoe box with flowers made from Dad's newspaper and lining the bottom with carpet samples Mom's left on the counter for weeks. It's easy to take things like that without Mom noticing.

LilyLee was always jealous of me wearing my mother's things. I'd come to school with a necklace with a tiny diamond hanging off it, or a yellow silk scarf that looked like it was stitched from Rumpelstiltskin's gold, and LilyLee would tell me how lucky I was that my mom didn't care about things like that.

"It's not that she doesn't care, it's that she doesn't notice," I'd say, but even though she's my best friend, LilyLee didn't understand the difference.

Before bringing the egg upstairs to my closet, I check the mailbox, looking for a note from LilyLee. I've been sending her postcards every other day, but there's nothing from her. Two weeks ago she sent a postcard of Boston Common and said she would feed the ducks for me. And a week before that she sent a postcard of some old-time movie star and a list of movies we should watch when she visits Labor Day weekend.

For the first time, I wonder if she'll even come.

"Is the mail working?" I ask my sisters.

"I got a package from Henry," Astrid says. We all pause at the name Henry. His name is a huge stop sign in the middle of our morning. Red and warning and dangerous to pass through.

"Quiet!" Marla says. She turns on the mixer, a rumbling sound meant to cover up the conversation. Nothing has ever made Mom angrier than when Astrid started going out with a boy named Henry last year.

Astrid presses her lips together.

"You're letting him send things here? What if Mom sees?" I say.

"When's the last time Mom left the house, even to check the mail?" Astrid says. It's a fair point, but still. Not worth the risk. It's bad enough that Eleanor has a secret boyfriend. Astrid shouldn't also be in contact with Henry. If Mom's ever going to get better, it will be because we've all been good. Doing all the things she hates will only make Mom sicker.

I think it but don't say it.

Eleanor looks up from her phone. "What should I wear to dinner at his birthday party?" She's missed the whole conversation, that's how much she must like the secret boyfriend. She hasn't told Marla and me his name. And if we asked whose birthday party she's going to, she'd make something up. But still.

Marla turns the mixer on even higher. She drops a bag of chocolate chips on the floor not once but three times. It doesn't make a very satisfying or loud sound, but I guess it makes Marla feel better.

"Maybe something green?" Astrid says.

Eleanor wrinkles her nose. This is not the answer she wanted. "Why?"

"I like green?" Astrid has already lost focus, and I think Eleanor and I are going to laugh about it, but we don't. Or I sort of do, but Eleanor wipes away a few tears.

"I need more help than that," she says in a small voice. She is starting to sweat. It always starts on her forehead; she can't hide the shine there. "I need someone who knows stuff."

What she means is: she needs a mom.

We all look at the stairs, the trail to our parents' room. Then we all look away, just as quickly.

There's nothing left to say, so everyone returns to our activities and the thoughts in our heads. It's the perfect time to sneak away with an egg.

The egg and I go into my closet. I hold it between my hands, cupping it. When the door's closed the light goes cozy and pink again, but the egg doesn't move.

Until it does.

It shakes and shudders.

It grows and cracks.

It breaks open.

I was thinking a creature of some kind would emerge, but sunshine is what bursts out of the shell. Beams of light, the same yellow as the yolk of an egg, the same sheen the whites have when one's first cracked open.

I reach my hands up to touch the beams as they shoot from the broken shell, and discover they have texture to them. They make my fingers tingle, almost putting my hand to sleep, but not quite. It's the feeling of a sparkle. The sunbeams sparkle against my hand. I've never felt a sparkle before. I like it.

I love it.

The closet doesn't flood with light. The beams stay independent, like lasers decorating the space, crisscrossing in the air above me and next to me and eventually through me, so that my middle, too, gets that sleepy, sparkly sensation.

The beams pick me up in the air and fly me around. They roll me, like I'm rolling down a hill, but I'm in the air, so it's smooth and strange instead of stumbly and awkward.

I never want to leave my closet.

Except that I want my sisters in here with me. I want to be all together. I don't want to be alone anymore.

And if Astrid's right, the closet could be even more incredible with all four of us in it, harnessing some kind of sister power.

So I leave the warm feeling, the sunbeams and their

pretty pattern, the unusual sensations, tickly and soothing at the same time. The trip in the sky, carried by sunbeams. I want to get my sisters in here with me. I want more eggs and more beams and more feelings of calm and happiness and easiness and thrill.

When I emerge from the closet, Astrid's already in my room.

"Priscilla," she says, a one-word sentence that says more than a whole paragraph could.

"I needed to," I rush to say.

"You have to come downstairs," she says. "Eleanor needs our help. Mom's roaming, but El needs to get to the birthday party."

"Whose birthday party?" I say, even though I know the answer. I want her to admit Eleanor does bad things too.

"You know whose," Astrid says. "Don't make it harder, okay? Having a secret boyfriend is making this tolerable for Eleanor. So."

"This is making it tolerable for me," I say, and gesture toward the closet door. Astrid sighs.

"I won't tell this time." She twists a silver-blond strand of hair around her thumb and releases it. It stays pin-straight, of course.

I step closer to my sister. She smells unusual: Like salt

and wind. Like the ocean and a roll in a meadow. Like a place we've never been.

I breathe it in deeply, so she knows that I know she's been in a closet today too.

eleven

"She's unwinding," Marla says.

Mom likes to "unwind" before dinner, which means she likes to open a bottle of wine and get the rest of us piled into the TV room to watch the Disney Channel for a while so she can enjoy her unwinding by herself.

The problem with Mom's unwinding is that we can't sneak outside when she's at the kitchen counter.

Actually, there are a lot of problems with Mom's unwinding, but most of them come after.

Eleanor's in a green dress, hiding in the downstairs bathroom. The dress cuts low, lower than anything I've seen her wear before. I want to put her in the running shorts and

T-shirt she wears for soccer, and some muddy sneakers.

She has a purse. Her hair is curling at the ends. She has lipstick on. No wonder she's hiding.

"We can't interrupt unwinding time," I say. We are having a sister meeting in the bathroom, with the faucet running hard and the fan making its too-loud noise. I don't know that any of this actually hides the sounds of our whispering, but we've agreed to at least pretend together that it does.

"You only need to get her out of the kitchen for a minute," Eleanor says. She's gripping her phone in one hand and the bottom of her dress with the other. She's near tears. I don't like this new side of Eleanor. Eleanor is supposed to be calm and eternally correct and sure.

"Don't upset Mom," Marla says. "Can't you wait until she's done? She'll fall asleep when she's done, probably." Marla's wringing her hands and has her Marla-pout on.

We don't know when she'll be done. Unwinding takes anywhere from a half hour to three hours, and there's no predicting it. There's no predicting Mom's moods.

"I'll do it," I say. "I'll distract her." I want them to look at me the way they did the other day in Eleanor's closet. Like I am old enough and solid enough to be a full-fledged sister, and not simply The Youngest or The Baby or Silly.

We concoct a plan where I distract Mom and lead her

up to my room. Marla will follow us up there to help out if I freeze and forget what to say and do, but she looks sour about it.

"You'd never do this for me," Marla whines. "You're such a kiss-up." I hate her voice when it sounds like this. Astrid is the lookout, staying down by the stairs to tell Eleanor when it's safe to sneak out. She'll cough really loud to cover the click of the front door closing.

When we get to the kitchen, Mom's unwinding with a photo album. I peek over her shoulder. The pictures are of Mom when she was Marla's age, and another little girl who looks a lot like me.

I elbow Marla, hoping she'll see the photos and start asking questions, so that I don't have to. Maybe I'm wrong and Mom has mentioned her sister before. Maybe we really are bad daughters who don't care about anything but ourselves, like Mom says when she's been drinking.

But Marla is too focused on Mom's face and the expressions passing across it, instead of what is causing those expressions to occur.

"Mom? Will you come to my room?" I say, like I'm supposed to. I step closer to her and ignore the way she smells. I want a better look at the pictures.

"Why?" Mom says.

I hadn't thought about an answer to that question. I

thought she'd follow me upstairs simply because I'd asked, even though that's never happened before.

Silly, Silly, Silly. I call myself the name I hate, as punishment.

"I have a bunch of questions about your sister," I say. It's not what I mean to say. But my mind gets too hyper and too hazy when Mom is sick, and I make terrible decisions. It's all queasy regret the moment the word *sister* comes out of my mouth.

"You saw her?" Mom says. Her voice is far away, except that it's right here. The strangeness of that gives me chills. New Hampshire gives me a chill in general. It is never hot here. Only ever warmish with a breeze. I want one hot day.

"You mentioned her. Is that her in the pictures?" I say. Marla stands next to me with her mouth open and her arms loose at her sides, like my stupidity is making her stupid too. I think I can hear Eleanor and Astrid mumbling in the bathroom, and I wish I could tell them to be quiet.

Mom rubs her temples. She takes a sip from her glass of wine. Then another. Her teeth are already stained a scary purplish color.

I try to guess at how she's feeling and how she'll respond. But there are a thousand options, and whichever one I think it will be is probably wrong. There's always some new response, some strange hiccup that I hadn't expected.

"She won't let me in," Mom says, her finger tracing the heart-shaped face of the girl in the pictures. "She won't come out. I can't get her." I feel my forehead scrunching up so much that I'm giving myself a headache. Or maybe Mom's giving me a headache.

"Can we talk about it in my room?" I try again, knowing full well it's a lost cause. I got distracted and sloppy and ruined everything. Typical.

"You don't have a sister," Marla says. "Mom doesn't have a sister." She elbows me without moving her gaze from Mom's drooping face.

"You think I didn't care enough about her?" Mom says, hearing something entirely different than what was said. "You think it was my fault?"

"No!" Marla says. "I don't know!" Mom gets off her stool and drains the rest of her wine. She wipes her mouth with the back of her hand. It's not very graceful. One of her feet hooks around the other, and she stumbles. "I didn't know," Marla says. I want to cover her mouth. I should say something so that Marla stops speaking, but I'm mute. "You've never mentioned her before."

"You think I forgot all about her," Mom says. "You think that's the kind of person I am!"

Mom's moving toward the cabinet that holds more bottles, and Marla steps in front of her, blocking her path.

It happens fast, while I'm trying to think of more words to get Mom calmed down or talking about something else, something less upsetting.

Marla takes one step closer to Mom, and Mom grabs Marla's wrists. One in each hand.

I look away.

I am the kind of sister who looks away.

Marla yelps, a surprised, animal sound, and I run up the stairs, straight into my closet.

twelve

I lie in the warm pink light of my closet for a long time. Nothing else in the room changes, only me.

When I come out, I knock lightly on the twins' door. It's dark. I stayed in the closet long past bedtime. Past whatever happened in the moments after Marla's terrible yelp.

Eleanor answers the door in her pink nightgown. The rest of us wear shorts and tank tops to bed, or worn-out pajama pants with Christmas trees on them, the kind we get some years from Dad. The years that Mom doesn't feel like doing Christmas, so Dad has to buy all the presents.

"I messed up," I say.

"No kidding. I didn't get to the birthday party. We were

all stuck here. And don't think we don't know what you were doing in your room."

"And Marla—," I say, wondering why Eleanor cares more about her secret boyfriend than she does about our sister.

"I'm mad at Marla, too, don't worry," Eleanor says, like I'm worried about sharing the blame. Sometimes I think Eleanor doesn't know me at all.

"Is she okay?" I say. Astrid rolls out of bed and stands in the doorway with Eleanor.

"She's Marla," Eleanor says with a cruel shrug. Eleanor's not that cruel, though. I have a feeling they don't know what happened.

I guess I don't really know what happened, either.

Maybe nothing happened. I didn't really see. Marla makes a big deal out of small things. Marla's been known to make loud noises in quiet moments, to exaggerate to get our attention.

"I'm sorry," I say. "I did everything wrong."

"I give up," Eleanor says, and she really does sound like she's given up. "Everyone can do whatever they want." It's the saddest thing I've ever heard Eleanor say. All she's ever cared about is telling us what to do and how to do it. All she's ever wanted are rules and for her sisters to follow them.

"I won't go in my closet anymore," I say, but I know

that's not true. If Eleanor is going to be sad and Mom-like, I'll need the closet even more. If I won't be allowed in their closet anymore, I'll need my own.

Astrid reaches out and touches my arm, the place where it bends.

"We don't know what your closet is for," Astrid says.

"It's for me!" I say, even though I know that's not what she's talking about.

"We don't know how it works. We understand Eleanor's. And we know mine is bad. And we know Marla's doesn't work. Yours is too mysterious. We'd tried it once a long time ago and it didn't work, but now it does and we don't know anything about what it does. Do you really want one more unpredictable thing in this house?" Astrid says. She's talking about Mom, of course, but ignoring the fact that something could be unpredictably wonderful, not only unpredictably awful.

"So you went in your closet and it felt funny?" I say, drastically changing what Astrid said. I don't want to call her closet the bad closet. I want to leave room for it to be something else.

"It was a long time ago," Astrid says. "And we didn't need another closet. It was ugly. It made things bad. Things we brought inside. And us. It made us bad, too."

I try to think through all the summers we've had here

to place which summer Eleanor and Astrid might have gone inside the bad closet. Which summer they acted bad or strange or unlike themselves.

I remember a week last summer when they tried Mom's wine. It was late at night and they were being loud in their bedroom, and when I walked in, Astrid was hugging a bottle and Eleanor was wearing sunglasses and a life vest. They moved in slow motion, and it took a lot of giggling and slurring for them to articulate that they wanted me to leave.

They never thanked me for not telling Mom and Dad.

"Was it last summer that you went in the bad closet?" I say, but Eleanor shakes her head to end that part of the conversation. She's mad at me and desperate to make sure I feel the deep, dark crevices of that anger and disappointment.

"All I wanted was to get out of this stupid house for five minutes. You had one small job and you couldn't even do that right," Eleanor says. I've never seen her like this, like Mom. Ready to explode with only a tiny push of an invisible button.

"I'm sorry. I saw these photos she was looking at and I got all weird and you know when I'm around Mom I can act sort of—"

"Silly, it's late," Eleanor says. "I'm tired. I had a bad night. You shouldn't be pretending you're, like, mature enough for this stuff. It's okay. We don't expect that from you. That's why we take care of you. Because you need us. And we thought you might be ready for more, but clearly, *clearly* you're not."

"Okay," I say. But it isn't.

thirteen

I go looking for Marla in the morning.

She's not in her sad, gray-walled room with its tarnished brass bed that she begged Dad for. She's not in the kitchen or the TV room. She's not on the porch next to Dad, stealing the comics section from his paper. She's not in the bathroom with the claw-foot tub that she likes to take long baths in. I think maybe I'll check in Mom's sewing room, but we're not supposed to go in there, and I don't want to get myself or anyone else into any more trouble. I even approach Mom and Dad's room, but I can hear Mom's heavy breathing, and I don't think she's awake.

Eleanor and Astrid have the television on downstairs. I

hear loud voices and cheesy music and the volume moving up and down every few seconds, because Eleanor likes it loud and Astrid likes it quiet. I should not sneak into their room without asking. I'm in more than enough trouble with Eleanor already.

But I have a creeping feeling about Marla, and I need to know where she is, I need to see that she's okay.

Guilt is this thing that feels gray and heavy. It's a cement wall between me and the rest of the world. Sleeping and eating and writing LilyLee are stuck on the other side, with me stranded over here, unable to do anything at all.

I'll do anything to tear it down.

So I head into Eleanor and Astrid's room. The beds are made. The shades are drawn. Eleanor's closet door is open, and nothing interesting is inside.

Astrid's closet door is closed.

I look under the beds and take an extra-long look at Eleanor's closet, in case somehow Marla is hiding in the back.

She isn't.

She is in Astrid's closet. The bad closet. Alone. I know it.

"Marla?" I say at the closet door.

"One second." Her voice sounds far away.

"Are you really in there?" It is a stupid thing to say, but I say stupid things when I'm nervous.

"One second. I promise, Sil," she says. Marla calls me Sil instead of Silly when she likes me, which is almost never. I stand outside the door with the world's straightest back and widest eyes.

I do not open the door. It's pretty possible that I don't want to go in there, curious or no.

The things Astrid said about her closet—vague half sentences—were creepy. Eleanor's mouth—the way it turned down and got crooked when she talked to me last night—was even scarier.

It would take a lot for Astrid to avoid something magical, I think. Eleanor likes night-lights when she's sleeping and flashlights when she's camping and explicit itineraries when she's doing anything else. But Astrid is her perfect counterpart. She likes playing hide-and-seek in pitch black and sleeping outside instead of in the tent and running off for a little while when we're on the beach, terrifying everyone but most especially Mom.

I'm not sure I want to see anything that Astrid is too scared to explore. Even if Marla likes it.

After all, Marla is odd. She likes poetry and worrying and the way things look in the rain. She likes Mom more than Dad. She likes eggs more than pancakes. She likes burnt toast and asparagus. She likes the New Hampshire house.

Of course she'd want to check out the bad closet, what-ever that means.

When Marla opens the door, the magic lingers, like with the other closets.

There are flowers on the floor. Not stems, only petals. Layers upon layers of them. They are so purple they are nearly black, and they have a mean-looking sheen.

There is what looks like a tiny house. Doghouse-size. Made of piles of stones. I think it would be hot to touch. Or very, very cold, maybe. There are wings flapping so fast that I can't see what's attached to them, but the wings are silver and look sharp. The closet walls are dripping a dark-pink fluid. It is thick and strange—not water or slime or pasta sauce. More like wax. Glowing, gorgeous, luxurious wax.

It is beautiful.

Not beautiful in a way I understand. But beautiful.

It looks the way I sometimes feel late at night when I don't want to think about Mom anymore—heavy and pur-ple and dripping and strange.

"Wow," I say. I'm not sure the word comes out, or if it's just my breath, which I can see in a blast of air, since it is freezing cold in the closet.

Marla holds one of the petals up to me, and I wish it would fade already. In my closet it would.

"You're keeping the magic alive," Marla says.

"What?"

"Touch this," she says. She looks focused, like she's solving a math problem, and I think if I obey she'll close the door and make it all go away. So I touch the petal.

It shimmies and shudders. It grows.

"It's you," Marla says. "Come farther in."

I step back instead. The edges of magic start to fade. I take another step back, and the sharp corners of the things in the closet blur. The too-strong, too-sharp, so-sweet-it-hurts smell of a thousand flowers grows fainter.

"No," I say. "It's not me." I take another step back. The magic recedes further. The petal in Marla's hand crumbles and disappears.

"You're what's special. I mean, me too, I think. But you most of all. It wasn't the combination of the four of us in Eleanor's closet that made it all better. It wasn't some sisterhood power. It was you."

I take four more steps back and everything else in the closet disappears, and we are looking at Astrid's normal, empty closet, and not at some awful, beautiful, weirdly familiar nightmare.

"I did it all on my own," Marla says. "No diorama. Just, like, me. It sort of . . . looks the way I feel."

My heart hiccups. The magic didn't stay, wasn't growing the way it seems to when I'm in the closets, when I'm in control. But still.

"I brought things inside late one night too. But I don't need to bring things in. I only need me and my feelings and that's it. I mean, I can't do it in the other closets. You can do special things in all the closets, I guess, but at least this one closet lets me do stuff. It's a way better closet than Eleanor's. It's like your closet, right?"

I don't like the way her Marla-feelings looked.

"No," I say. "It's not anything like mine."

"Well. I wouldn't know," Marla says. "You haven't invited me in yours."

Her hand touches my forearm, and I can't believe how icy it is. So cold it's nearly hot, like I'd imagined the stone house might be. Right on that strange and mysterious line where the two extremes become one.

"Are you okay?" I say, because she doesn't seem the same.

"It's so cozy in there," Marla replies, which is not at all true. "I wish I could make the magic stay. Make it stronger. Use it in all the closets and be in control all the time. I hate that you're able to do things I can't do. Do you focus your mind? Did you know it was you that made things grow and move and become even more magical?"

"I'm not sure I'm anything special," I say. If I was so powerful, I wouldn't have let Marla be alone with Mom yesterday and I wouldn't have ruined Eleanor's night and I wouldn't feel the way I do right now—small and breakable.

"Eleanor and Astrid don't have what you have. Or what we have," Marla says. "They have their twin thing and Eleanor's closet, but they need those dioramas. You're so used to thinking they're the best, you haven't even considered that maybe they're not." She rubs her hands together like a villain in a movie, so I take one of her hands to make it stop.

"That buzzing thing in there looked sharp. Like it could hurt you."

Marla nods. "It hurts a little, I guess, if it flies into you. But it's so pretty. And funny. It, like, teases, you know?"

I think of the lightbulb that shrank and turned pink and playful with me. "Sure," I say. "I mean, I guess. It looked sort of mean. But it sounds like it's, um, nice?"

Marla's other cold, cold hand grabs mine. I don't want to tell her how scared I am, but I can barely feel my fingers. I don't like any of it. I feel the opposite of the delicious UnWorry in my closet.

"Please don't tell," she says. Her eyes are too dark for her face, too dark for the sister I've known for all of my eleven years. And her hands are too cold to belong to a girl, especially in the summertime, but I try to ignore both of those things, because her voice is so soft and nice and she has that look of calm that I know I've felt before. "I need something that's mine too," she says.

I can't argue. Especially not after last night.

We eat breakfast, and I try to talk to Marla about the bad closet and about what happened with Mom last night and about how to stay safe and have magic and how we should tell Astrid and Eleanor about what we saw.

"Beach!" Marla says in nonresponse, a cheerleader all of a sudden. Usually when we go to the lake during the summer, Marla sits on the dock and rips splinters of wood from its surface and complains about sand being in her sandwich. Today she is too eager and in this old bathing suit that must have been Eleanor's or Astrid's before hers. It seems especially cruel to get bathing suits as hand-me-downs.

"We should ask Mom if it's okay," I say. She has strange and specific rules about the lake, and new rules pop up all the time. We can't go before noon or after three. We can't go with boys. We have to be no more than five feet away from one another at all times. We have to bring a cell phone.

Asking Mom if something's okay is Marla's favorite thing to do, but she doesn't seem that interested right now. She shrugs and leaves a note on the counter, but the note says we're going to the store for sodas, not to the lake for a swim. It's a side of Marla I've never seen before.

"What do you think Eleanor's secret boyfriend looks like?" I say on the walk to the beach, wondering if maybe I can start a conversation in one place and make it go somewhere else. Marla shrugs. She seems already irritated by the sun and the sand the moment we get to the lake.

Whatever calm she got from the closet is fading fast. I try again.

"I haven't heard from LilyLee in kind of a while. Do you think she has some new best friend?" I say. Marla shrugs.

"Do you miss anything from home?" I say. Marla shrugs.

"Did you ever hear of 'The Twelve Dancing Princesses'? It's one of Dad's fairy tales," I say. Marla sighs and tugs at the bottom of her bathing suit.

"Why didn't Mom tell us she has a sister?" I say, since being subtle isn't getting me anywhere.

Marla gives me a funny look. "Had a sister, I think," she says.

"Oh." Of course I know she's right, but I hadn't thought about it in stark terms, and the word sort of bowls me over. *Had* a sister. It's an awful thing, the past tense.

"Let's go in," she says.

No one else is on our patch of sand. This little area of

the lake has always been only ours. We can see other families playing on the other side of the lake, at the other end of the strip of beach, closer to the lifeguard, or their own private coves, but we can't be part of them.

Marla runs to the lake and I follow, splashing in behind her. She scowls at me when I kick too hard at the water and it hits her face. Marla's not much of a swimmer, so she stands in the water, up to her waist, and watches me bob up and down in an unofficial stroke I call Mermaid Swimming.

I'm out of breath quickly and return to stand next to her. Our shoulders are burning, for sure.

"She started talking about it when we moved here," Marla says. "About her sister, I mean. But you know she says so many things that don't make sense. . . ." She takes a few steps back, closer to shore, so the water is barely at her knees. "I don't think we want to know what happened."

"Why? I want to know everything that's happened to everyone," I say. I mean it, too. I want to know about Mom and Dad and my sisters, but also LilyLee and her family and also the fairy tales and myths and fables in Dad's office and the people on the other side of the lake and Astrid's old secret boyfriend and Eleanor's new one. I want to know it all.

"There's probably a reason no one's told us," Marla says. "And anyway, Mom needs her privacy."

These are Mom's words, not Marla's. Mom says them whenever we're bugging her to tell us more about when she was growing up, or asking her if we can play in her room or use the sewing machine. "I need my privacy," Mom will say, rubbing her eyes and raising her shoulders way up to her ears.

"You're not worried about anything?" I say. "Like that maybe the New Hampshire house is making everything worse? I mean, last night was bad. With you and her." I dip back under the water, becoming a mermaid for three amazing seconds before popping back up to the surface. Mom doesn't like us going underwater, but she's never at the lake to stop us anymore.

"It was fine," she says. "Mom's really stressed out from the move." We moved almost two months ago now, so that explanation seems off, but I don't say anything.

Marla's sick of the water already and mumbles something about sunblock and sitting down. We don't have towels, so I think we'll go to the dock, but she plops herself on the beach, a terrible idea in a wet bathing suit.

I sit in the sand next to her and bury my feet in the wet parts. It's sort of like after a decade of coming to the beach in the summers, we've suddenly forgotten how to do it right.

Like Mom and her failed French toast.

It all has me feeling limp.

Marla lies back in the sand, and I can't imagine the trouble that's going to cause her already messy hair. Sand will get knotted in with the rest of the tangles, and she'll be washing it out for days. She doesn't seem to care. Like a starfish, she spreads all her limbs out wide, and I notice something on her wrist.

I should have noticed it in the closet or on the walk down here or while we were wading in the lake, but I get so tired from watching Mom's every move and expression and skin-tone change that I forget to pay attention to much else. Especially when it comes to Marla.

"What's that?" I say, pointing.

Marla grabs her wrist with her other hand like she's scared of letting me see, until she remembers it's just the new bracelets circling the delicate bone. There are five of them, beaded and sparkling. Different colors, and I can see that each bracelet has a different word beaded on: KINDNESS, COMPASSION, BRAVERY, HONESTY, LOVE.

"Mom gave them to me last night. A special present," Marla says. "She got them last time she was in California."

Mom has gone to California a few times, and Arizona twice and Minnesota and Boston and Florida. She goes Away and gets better. But after a few months or a year, she always gets worse again.

"That's not how it goes in fairy tales," I said to Dad

when he first explained it to me. That someone can get better and things can be happily-ever-after and then get just as bad or even worse later.

That was a long time ago now. I've understood the not-happily-ever-after-ness for a while.

"What do the bracelets mean?" I ask Marla. I think I see something under the bracelets too. A shadow of something on her skin. A discoloration. A shade of light blue that doesn't quite fit in with the rest of Marla's arm.

"Mom says they mean that we're all doing our best," Marla says. She spins them around, and I lose sight of the thing I thought I saw underneath.

"Can I have one?" I ask. I like the way they catch the light, the same way the ripples on the lake do, creating little specks of sparkle and shine. I want the one that says BRAVERY, but Marla gives me KINDNESS. I'm not sure what that means, but I assume it's either the one she thinks I need or the one she thinks she already has conquered.

"Poor Mom," Marla says. "The house makes her sad. She said that the other day. She thought it would make her happy, but it doesn't." I hate the way Marla takes Mom's side in everything, even now. I'm boiling, and it's not from the sun. "You really should be nicer to her," Marla concludes.

I leave Marla on the beach. It's a long walk back, but not long enough to walk off my steaming madness at what she said to me. The bracelet feels more like a demand now. A really, really unreasonable one.

~⁓~

When I get home, Eleanor, Mom, and Dad are on a bike ride.

"Mom went on a bike ride?" I say.

"She did," Astrid says.

"I'm worried about everything," I say. And I am—I'm worried about Marla in Astrid's closet and whatever was underneath her bracelets, and Mom riding a bike, and the bracelets themselves with their too-encouraging words, and the clank of bottles when we take out recycling every other night. And the sister Mom used to have but doesn't have anymore.

"I have an idea. Don't tell Eleanor and Marla, okay?" Astrid says. She doesn't tell me everything's going to be fine, and that's why I love her the most.

Astrid takes a white tulip from a vase in the kitchen. Dad must have bought Mom a bouquet, and that should be a good sign, but in our family it's a bad one. Dad buys flowers for Mom when he's scared.

"Put the tulip on the floor," she says when we're inside my closet with it moments later. "Or pin it to the wall, if you want. That could be cool." There are a few rogue pushpins already shoved into the wall, and she nods to them. I guess that means I should go for it, so I stab the stem of the tulip with a pin and let it hang. If it stays for too long, I'm afraid a petal or two will fall off and what was once perfect will be ugly.

I want it to stay beautiful and full. I want it to be fuller, bigger, more alive.

Astrid grins and closes the door.

"Just wait," she says. So we do.

"For what?" I say.

"That."

The flower I pinned to the wall is growing. Even after what I've seen the last few days in the closets, it's alarming to watch a small white tulip grow to the size of my entire body in under five minutes.

"I came in here with one earlier," Astrid says. Usually I am the one who sneaks into her room, not the other way around. I like being on this side of things. "Nothing. And now you're here. And look at what happens. It's you. You do this."

"I bet there is some special power to us being together. When the girls get back, we'll see how much bigger it can get."

"I bet you can do even more," Astrid says.

I touch the stem, and the whole thing shivers and more petals sprout so that the bloom widens, becomes more spectacular. Astrid smiles and touches the tulip, but it does nothing under her hand. It stays large and changed from the closet, but nothing extra happens.

Maybe it is me.

Maybe.

"It's okay to have something the rest of us don't have," Astrid says. "We may look surprised, but we're not." She doesn't seem defeated like Marla did earlier or angry like Eleanor. She is Astrid—gentle and distracted by beautiful things and wise but totally unaware of it.

But the thing is, even though I think maybe she's right, I don't feel powerful at all. I feel the opposite. Small. Awed. Drowning in awesomeness. I touch the stem of the huge tulip and it twists like a corkscrew. It grows like a vine all over the room, more and more tulips shooting out of the one stem.

I want to tell her about Marla and the magic she found in Astrid's closet, but I know I'm not supposed to. Keeping Marla's secret is the least I can do for her right now.

Astrid puts her palm over my hand and holds it to one of the flowers. The petals all open and close in unison. Something like a song comes out. Like a music box or the handbells that they use in church.

It's so incredible that I cry. Choking tears that Astrid tries to squeeze out of me with a massive bear hug, but I can't stop. It's so astonishing my body can't handle it.

It feels like we are inside a flower. Inside a singing flower that I am somehow in charge of, that I made sing.

"How'd you come up with that?" Astrid says. She's crying too. It must be too pretty for either of us to manage.

"I didn't."

"You have a spark," Astrid says, all wise and serious, and I think someday she'll be one of those people who sits on mountaintops with their legs crossed and tells everyone else the secrets of life. "Eleanor knows it too," she says. She looks at me hard, like she's trying to outstare the part of me that thinks Eleanor hates me, finds me insignificant, wishes I weren't her sister. "It's hard for her," she concludes, and that's all she's going to say on the subject.

The petals grow larger, thicker, the song a little louder, and for a moment I feel a ping of terror that they could suffocate us, but Astrid's body doesn't hiccup with fear, and I know if there were a reason to be scared, she'd let me know.

I like the feeling of the petals. They are sturdy and soft at the same time. I wrap myself in one of them, and Astrid does the same. I feel safe and protected for the first time ever in the New Hampshire house.

"Can we stay in here all day?" I say. "What else can we bring in here?"

"It's better than the world out there," Astrid says.

"It *is*." I unwrap myself and grab another silky-smooth curved triangle. Decide to hoist myself up, up, up, and see what happens. The petal smells perfect.

The song shifts a little, quiets and complicates itself, the different blooms singing different notes.

I grab on to one of the lower-hanging petals. It's hard to climb. It swings a little when I shimmy. Every inch I travel, the farther away all our problems are. If I climb to the top, maybe I'll be more like LilyLee—small and light and kind of clueless. I wouldn't mind not knowing some things, come to think of it.

All that time wanting to know all the secrets, and now I wish I knew less.

"Where do you think you're going?" Astrid calls out. She's laughing, and I tell her to grab on and climb up with me. I wait while she tries, but she can't seem to get a grip. When I grab the petals they help me, but when she does, they reject her.

"It's not hard," I say, swinging a few petals farther up.

"It won't let me," Astrid says. "I'm only really good for the dioramas, I guess." If it were Marla in here she'd throw a fit, but with Astrid there's a shrug in her voice. She doesn't need the same things the rest of us need. She has a whole wild world in her head, a perfect escape always at the ready. "I like watching you, though," she says, and I'm surging with sisterly love, which is the best kind of love.

I take another petal, wrap my legs around a new stem, and grunt as I shift into a slightly higher atmosphere. "What if I want to stay in here forever, climbing into, like, infinity?" I say. "What if climbing this flower is the greatest thing ever, and I have tons of energy and could keep going all day?"

"Then I'm pretty sure it will never end," Astrid says. "From what I've seen, the closets give you what you need. What you ask for."

"And your closet?" I say. I can't tell her about Marla, but maybe I can make her figure it out on her own. Maybe I can hint about what happened in there.

"It's different," Astrid says. And then in a much tinier voice, "I don't know."

I get a spike of fear in my chest, but it disappears pretty fast in here. Outside the closet, the fear can last all day. The dread. In here it comes up and fades away in almost the same breath.

I keep climbing, and Mom's KINDNESS bracelet falls off my wrist and onto one of the petals.

"I can't wait to show LilyLee all this," I call down. I think of the postcard I will try to write LilyLee tonight and how I'll lead her in here when she visits at the end of the summer. The adventures we'll have.

"I think it's only for us sisters," Astrid says. "Maybe don't worry so much about LilyLee."

"I guess." I'm getting a little tired. The fear didn't last, but it took some of my energy with it, so I look above me to see how much farther there is to go. What had looked infinite before is now closing in. A ceiling of white petals is the exact right distance away from me. I've reached the top, because I want to reach the top.

Astrid is right. It is giving me what I want.

I look for a way down. Climbing up the petals was relatively easy; figuring out a way down is much harder. I kick my feet around until they find a sturdy bit of stem. I wrap my legs around it and work my way down, gripping petal after petal.

When I reach the place where the bracelet fell off, I blink about eight hundred times to make sure I'm seeing things right. The tiny blue circle of plastic beads has turned into a rope of sapphires. Massive, tennis-ball-size gems, in long strands braided together and hanging all the way from the flower to the ground, which seems like it must be miles below, but it's hard to keep perspective from up here. It hurts my fingers, the sharpness of the stones, but they're so beautiful and sparkly it doesn't matter. I'm climbing down a jeweled rope. In a tiny universe of giant white flowers. Life couldn't get much better.

Eleanor's closet made me feel safe. My closet makes me feel like I'm on an adventure.

Astrid beams at me as I swing to the bottom. "Where did that come from?" she says. She gets up and comes over to touch the jewels. "You're getting good at this, huh?"

"Some bracelet Mom gave Marla. From Florida. Or Minnesota? I don't remember. From one of her places," I say. I don't think Astrid will like it, and I'm right.

"Oh."

"I had it on."

"Yeah . . ." Astrid stops fingering the sapphires and puts her hands in her pockets. Astrid never wants to talk about Mom.

I guess only Marla really likes talking about Mom, and I don't understand the way she talks about her, so it doesn't count.

"I'm sorry," I say. I let go of the sapphire rope.

It's beautiful, but that doesn't matter.

"Let's go," Astrid says. She goes to the door, and I want to weep, losing all the prettiness. "That's enough for today."

If I hadn't brought Mom's bracelet in, we could have stayed all afternoon.

fourteen

I'm sad about leaving the closet, so Astrid suggests ice cream.

Everyone's back home and obviously Eleanor is on board, since her secret boyfriend works there. Marla doesn't want the three of us going alone, so she comes too, even though she doesn't like ice cream.

It is so like Marla, to be into crackers and sips of Mom's coffee and the stinkiest cheeses, but to hate ice cream.

"Don't say anything strange," Eleanor says. "Don't tell him anything about home, okay? Actually, don't say you're my sisters at all. He doesn't know I have a family."

"Everyone has a family," I say. Eleanor's all nervous

energy. She's not as sweaty as she gets around Mom, but she's biting her fingernails and walking too fast.

"I mean, he knows I theoretically have one. But I don't need him to be thinking about it all the time."

"Don't be a weirdo," Astrid says. She gives Eleanor the heaviest kind of look, and I know that even though she has met the secret boyfriend, Eleanor didn't introduce her as her twin. We can get away with that sort of thing in my family. We don't look so sister-y, even the twins.

"I don't mind you guys coming, but it's my world, you know? I want my own space that isn't all . . . sullied."

We are the thing that makes Eleanor imperfect. We are the smudge on the clear, clean window.

I'm hot with fury.

I don't say anything. But I walk with stiff limbs and a tight chest and angry, shallow breaths. I'm light-headed and aching and don't even really want ice cream anymore.

When we get there, the first thing Eleanor does is lean across the counter.

"Hey you," she says, in this voice I've never heard that is too husky. Marla rolls her eyes.

The boyfriend tucks some of Eleanor's hair behind her ear and she kisses his cheek.

He's not as cute as I'd hoped. His arms aren't the right size for his body; they are a little too long and a little too skinny. He has braces and squinty eyes. But the way those eyes look at Eleanor is good.

I am torn between letting her have him and ruining it all.

I'm fighting back some evil side of myself that I didn't know I had. The evil side is winning. It's like I'm so tired from trying to be good that I've worn myself out and don't have it in me anymore.

"I'm Priscilla," I say, popping up next to Eleanor. I'm pumping with energy. Everything that's been wrong and confusing and frustrating is gathering and focusing in on this one moment. "One of Eleanor's sisters."

I hate myself for doing it. But I also hate Eleanor for making me want to do it.

She coughs. She blushes. She steps on my foot so hard the pain screeches in my body.

"Hey, cool," the secret boyfriend says. "I had no idea you had sisters. I would have made sure to send you home with extra ice cream every day." He winks at me.

"Maybe I wanted all the ice cream for myself," Eleanor says. She's saying it to both him and me, and I wonder how much damage this is all causing. I'm desperate to be close to her and dying to hurt her the way she's hurting me, all at the same time.

"I like raspberry chocolate chip," I say. He scoops me

and Eleanor overfull cones and loads on the sprinkles. Eleanor's isn't bigger or sprinklier than mine, and I can see her noticing that. She licks the cone halfheartedly and doesn't take her eyes off her secret boyfriend as he gets cones for Marla and Astrid.

Marla nibbles at her boring vanilla and we sit, all four of us, at a table in near silence.

"You couldn't let me have one thing?" Eleanor says when the secret boyfriend is busy helping someone else.

"You still have him." I take a huge bite of ice cream and it freezes my teeth, gives me a monster shiver.

"I'm sharing him now, I guess. I'm going to have to tell him about the family," Eleanor says. Something terrible has taken over her face. "I'm going to have to tell him why he can't come over and visit with all my adorable sisters. You know, you never used to be a huge brat. You used to get it. You used to—"

"You used to do a lot of things differently too," I say. I pull my shoulders down and back. I stick out my chest and wipe ice cream off my chin. I don't look away from her gaze, even though it hurts so much for her to hate me in this moment. I care and don't care.

Eleanor goes back to the counter and makes a big show out of playing with her secret boyfriend's hair. He feeds her a bunch of different flavors from tiny plastic spoons, and I get it, she has something special and new and lovely and we don't.

"I'd have done it if you didn't," Marla whispers in my ear before we head home. She bumps her hip against mine, and I know she's saying it to make me feel good, but it feels so, so sour.

We walk like that, me and Marla side by side and Eleanor and Astrid a few steps in front of us, and even though I was so close to being one of them, I'm now on a team with Marla, and I know for sure that I am one hundred percent incapable of doing anything right.

"We should have gotten a cone for Mom," Marla says, like it wouldn't have melted on the walk home. "She loves Oreo ice cream. That would have made her day."

None of us say anything.

Marla looks from me to Astrid to Eleanor and back again. She starts kicking stones when she realizes we're not going to respond.

Everything about the walk home hurts: My flip-flop breaks, so I have to hobble with one shoe on and one off and pebbles keep sticking their sharpest edges into my bare heel. The sun is strong this time of day, and my scalp hurts from the beginning of a burn there.

Marla shifts into a terrible mood, and she keeps moving her bracelets around, repositioning them over and over.

There's still a patch of wrong-colored skin underneath them. Every step closer we get to the house, the more groan-y and impossible she gets.

The twins don't seem to notice. I keep almost telling them to look at Marla's wrist, but I'm too scared to talk to Eleanor now that I've ruined everything. So the bracelets stay on and I don't get a good look at whatever's happening underneath them.

"It's so UNFAIR!" Marla yells, so sudden my heart does that jumping-then-dropping thing it does when I'm swinging too high on the swing set by our old school. She punches her thigh with her fist. "I try so hard! I try so, so, so, so, so hard! And none of you care! All you can talk about are closets and boyfriends and stupid stuff that doesn't matter. And I don't get anything, even though I try the hardest and do the most and love her the deepest and understand her the best!" Marla's not looking at us, but at the rest of the world—the giant pine trees and the pine needles covering the pavement and the mountains that are so far in the distance they almost look like fog.

We don't rush at Marla. We would, if that's what she needed, but it's not. We don't contradict her either, because in some ways she's right. We stay quiet and let her yell at the ground and the sky and the too-happy-looking clouds.

When she's all out of tears and words, we sit on the side

of the road for a moment and catch our breath. We're all four of us a little teary and strange. Too tired to keep walking, too overwhelmed to speak about it.

"We can tell Dad that Mom needs to go Away again," Eleanor says at last.

"No!" Marla interrupts before the sentence is even over. "Don't send her away! Why do you always want to send her away?" She is going to spiral into another freak-out if we don't nod our heads and keep walking, so that's what we do. For Marla.

It's a slow street. There aren't many cars. And it feels good to be shoulder to shoulder for a few minutes, without speaking.

There was a summer Mom was doing really well, and she took us to get ice cream every day, and we would sing songs on the walk home in loud voices. Mom would wave at trucks until they honked their horns for us, and we were raucous and ridiculous. I wonder if we're all thinking about that right now.

fifteen

Mom collects fabric. She once made a pink sundress for my teddy bear and a wedding gown for my favorite doll and a wool coat for my stuffed cat because I was worried he was getting cold in the winter months. Those are things that happened, even though they don't fit in with the Way Things Are Now.

We're not allowed in the sewing room, but the door's open and when we walk by it we see Mom's in there. I wish I could say she's fallen asleep in the chair or on the little couch she does the hand-stitching on. But that is not the case. She's on the floor. Her legs are splayed. It is a terrible, sudden kind of sleep. She's right in front of the sewing room closet, like she'd been pulling at the door and fell asleep from the effort.

I see her first. "Mom!" I exclaim, which brings Marla immediately to my side with Eleanor and Astrid not far behind.

"Oh," Astrid says. "Oh. Oh."

Eleanor puts two fingers on Mom's neck and the fingers of her other hand on Mom's wrist like she's some kind of doctor, and I don't think I'll ever be as old and together and sure as Eleanor.

"Do we need to call 911?" I say. It seems like the right thing to say. Like maybe I can be good in this situation too, but Eleanor shakes her head, and I guess she already knows what's going on.

"She's napping. We'll let her nap."

"We should tell Dad," Astrid says, but she's stepping aside, away from the situation. She picks at a piece of floral wallpaper that's starting to become unglued.

"No!" Marla says.

"Astrid, take the girls into my closet," Eleanor says.

"Now?" Astrid says.

"Now."

Eleanor is a boulder. She won't even look our way. She's wholly focused on Mom and her pulse and propping her up and checking the mug on the table to see what's in it. We are useless, compared to her.

"We can go to the mountains," Astrid says. She takes a diorama that's in the sewing room, one she gave Mom, who loves mountains, allegedly.

I don't know what Mom loves anymore. Not us, I don't think.

I erase that thought as quickly as possible. Thank myself for not saying it out loud.

～๛

The mountains are nice. They shimmer into existence a few moments after we enter the closet, diorama in hand. For a moment, they're transparent and not real, but they quickly become solid and real and enormous.

They are purple and covered in glitter. Exactly the kind of magical place I've been hoping to visit since I first went in the closet with the park diorama.

They sparkle *hard*.

They sparkle enough to make us laugh and wonder at the prettiness and want to stay in the closet all night.

We lie beneath them, in their shadows. If we were in my closet, I'd want to climb them, I'd want to go on an adventure on their glittering slopes. But Eleanor's closet is for feeling at home. Ladybugs swarm our knees and give us tiny ladybug kisses. An owl with huge eyes settles on a rock nearby. He doesn't squawk or flap or anything. He watches.

It is weird to think of an owl being sort of like a parent, so I don't say it out loud, but that's probably what I need, so it's what the closet is providing.

"Let's stay here," I say

"Maybe we really should," Astrid says. I had expected her to say no.

"Eleanor would hate it." I feel like I should stand up for Eleanor, after what I did to her today.

"Eleanor doesn't want to be one of us," Astrid says. She doesn't take her eyes from the top of the mountain, a place that glints in the sun.

My stomach turns and wails. "We should check on Mom," I say. "We should check on Eleanor. She shouldn't be doing that alone. We shouldn't be in here while she's out there. She's fourteen. She's not a doctor." I'm scared for her. We are making so many mistakes.

Astrid looks farther up, past the mountaintop. Far, far away.

"Don't you think Mom would want to see this?" Marla whispers. Astrid is so distracted watching strange yellow clouds bounce in the sky that she doesn't react.

"Sure," I say, but I don't know what Mom likes or wants.

"I'm going to bring a little bit of the dirt out," Marla says. "Show her how it sparkles. I won't tell her where it's from. Yet. But she probably needs to see something really beautiful right now. I think it will help."

"Maybe?" I can't imagine a handful of dirt causing any real trouble, so I keep my mouth closed and let her do it.

"We could stay," Astrid says. "I meant it, earlier. Maybe it would actually be better for us."

"Better to never go back to the real world?" Marla says. Her voice wobbles.

"They'd forget us after a while," Astrid goes on. "We've noticed that if we stay for a long time, we sort of . . . fade. Like, once Eleanor went in by herself in the morning, and by dinnertime Mom and Dad seemed foggy about her. Like they couldn't quite think of her name, and they didn't ask where she was."

"That sounds terrifying," I say.

She shrugs, like a slow fade away from everyone's memory is no big deal. "Yeah, I mean, sort of. Yeah," Astrid says, like I'm not understanding something. Marla doesn't say anything at all, and that's even worse. "It's nice, though, to think you could disappear for a while. And when Eleanor came back out, it was fine." Astrid is so pale and spacey anyway, she's always been half faded. She's never fully there.

"I don't want to fade away," I say. I touch Astrid's shoulder and she clicks back into herself, the moment over. She shakes her head, undoing some kind of dizziness that was in her brain, and I dig my fingers into her arm to keep her here, unfaded. Marla clings to the scoop of dirt that she thinks will cure Mom.

"Yeah, of course," Astrid says. "Me neither. Let's go help Eleanor. You're right. Of course you're right."

When we step out of the closet, Marla opens her hand to make sure the rocky dirt kept its magic.

It didn't.

Her hand is empty. The diorama's intact and simply a diorama again. The world is magic-less and Marla's face is hopeless, like she really thought Mom was going to be cured by a pile of glittering dirt.

I'm starting to think Mom's not going to be cured by anything at all.

"I'll think of something else," Marla says. "She'll be okay."

"*We'll* be okay," Astrid says.

I swallow nothing, hard.

sixteen

Eleanor is under her covers. All the way under. It's a signal that we shouldn't ask her what happened.

The sewing room door is closed. So is our parents' bedroom door. It must have gone badly, while we were at the mountain, letting Eleanor deal with it all by herself. No wonder she wants to pretend we don't exist.

I fall asleep quickly, once I'm in bed. I'm light-headed after the closet, the memory of Mom asleep on the floor and Marla's disappointment fading into nothingness.

Mom's still sleeping in the morning when I get up.

Dad's hunched over some huge book in the never-used dining room. "I'm reading about demons," he says.

"Demons?" I sit on one of the straight-backed chairs and look around the bottom floor of the house, as far as I can see from here, for signs that my sisters are awake and about. I think they're awake, but right now they're nowhere to be found.

"And deals with the devil. And tortured souls. And witches," Dad says. "Anything that makes good things go bad."

"Why?" I think it's because he's trying to figure out what's wrong with Mom too, but Dad mumbles something about his upcoming semester at the university and some unit he's going to do, and we don't end up having a real conversation.

"Stories are the most important, useful things we have to understand the world around us," Dad says finally. This he makes eye contact on, and I wonder if he could be right.

"Will you tell me more about 'The Twelve Dancing Princesses'?" I say.

"Hm?"

"The story? With the shoes? And the closets?"

Dad puts down his demon book for a minute. He flips through his legal pad like he's looking for something. He adjusts his glasses because he's serious about the situation.

"I made a list of stories and fables and myths about sisters for you," Dad says. "That's not the only one about siblings." This is typical Dad. Not quite understanding me but really, truly believing that he does. The smile on his face is all kinds of proud of himself, and I know he thinks he gets me, and I don't want to take that away from him.

"Wow. Thanks," I say.

"We're two peas in a pod." Dad emits a happy sigh, and I wonder if this is the only time all day either of us will be really happy. Who knows what else might happen to make the house sad later today? "We both really get how to look for answers. We're both curious. We both know the stories in these books are more than pretend. They're real, they have real things to teach us. Maybe you'll be a professor like me someday. What do you think, Silly?"

"Professor Silly," I say, hating it.

"I know things don't always make sense," Dad says. He's taken off his glasses, which means he's settling in for an important talk. "I know you're looking for answers to hard questions. But things are getting better now, and I think with how strong our family is and how smart and curious you are, it will all start to make sense for you. The world."

"You think the world will start to make sense." I want him to hear how he sounds. His big proclamations. The way he's gripping the sides of his books like they are anchors, life rafts, in a stormy sea. Doesn't he hear how hollow it all is?

"Now that we've moved here and Mom's getting better."

He smiles to himself and puts his glasses back on, conversation over.

There are so many things to say that I go mute. It's annoying, how that happens. The more things I want to say, the less I actually can. Eleanor's not like this. She gets an uppity, fast-talking voice when she needs to speak her mind. And Marla yells out her temper tantrums. Astrid writes long letters when she's upset.

I'm Silly. I say nothing, but I blush and look at the clock, which tells me it is way, way too late for Mom to still be asleep.

It's terrifying that Dad thinks Mom is doing better. If he doesn't see how bad things are, what are we supposed to do? I think about the mountains and the idea to escape there, and I think Dad would be the first to forget us.

Or Mom, if she'd been drinking all day.

I guess they'd both forget us.

I feel like I have the flu. A very sudden, very painful flu.

"Speaking of sisters, where are mine?" I say. I can't sit here with him pretending Mom's getting better when every day she's getting a little bit worse.

"Let's see. The beach maybe? Eleanor went to get ice cream. Which is funny—it's a little early for ice cream," Dad says like it's only occurred to him this moment.

"And Mom?" I say, hoping he'll admit how worrisome it is that she's sleeping.

"I'm sure she's reading or something," he says. "Anyway, I should get to work, chickadee. You'll hold down the fort for me? I'm going to the office."

He doesn't have to go to the office. It's summer. He could do his research right here. But he wants to leave too. We all need to leave sometimes.

He abandons most of his papers on the table, so when he's out the door I look through them. There are notes about everything from evil witches in Eastern European fairy tales to Bible verses about the devil to something called *The Metamorphosis*.

Dad likes reading and pondering and note-taking and concluding things from those books but never actually looking at what's happening in real life. It's sort of sad if I think too much about it.

I have an idea.

I rip a bunch of pages out of a copy of *Grimm's Fairy Tales*. Dad has a million copies; he won't miss this one.

I head to the basement. I know exactly what I'm looking for.

In the pile of discarded toys that we moved from Massachusetts to New Hampshire for no reason at all, I discover our old Barbies. Twelve of them. Mom would be livid if she knew we had twelve Barbies, but Dad always used to buy them for us when she was Away.

I come across Halloween costume tiaras and never-used ballet slippers and a pair of pink heels I'm sure Mom never wore but that maybe princesses could have worn. I bring a bowl of water that I hope will turn into a lake, because as I read the pages I ripped out of the book—the story of "The Twelve Dancing Princesses"—I learn that they took a boat across a lake to make it to the dance. I find one toy boat. It's small and plastic, and we probably used to play with it in the tub.

The fairy tale also says the sisters floated by trees of gold and silver, and I think of the gold in Eleanor's hair that one morning, and wonder if maybe we really *are* those princesses.

Of course I know we're not, but I wonder what it would feel like, for an afternoon, to live that story instead of our own.

I bring the tiaras and shoes and Barbies and book pages and everything else I can gather up from the fairy tale into the closet. I hang silver and gold chains from the hooks that used to be used for coats. I use some of Astrid's supplies and hang tinsel and sheer fabrics from the closet bar and place the bowl of water on the ground and float the little blue ship in it. It rocks back and forth.

I almost close the door and enter the world alone, but I don't. I miss my sisters. Even Marla, who is impossible and scaring me, but is one of us.

If I am going to travel inside a fairy tale, I want my sisters with me.

I close the closet door and wait on the stairs for Marla and Eleanor and Astrid to come home.

Mom wanders out of her bedroom after a few minutes, and I go cold and tense. I try not to smell her. I try not to look directly at her.

"Where are your sisters? You should all be together!" Mom says instead of hello, because somehow by sitting on the stairs alone I've done something terribly wrong. She's screeching, and I don't know why. It's frightening in the way that being lost in the woods is frightening. I don't know what's coming next. There might be bats or owls or a ditch or it might be fine, there might be a lit-up cottage with something baking inside right around the corner.

"I don't know, I got up late and—"

"What's wrong with you? We came here to be a family, and you're doing a terrible job! You're not all taking care of each other!" she screams. My heart's pounding. If anyone's doing a terrible job, it's her. My mouth is aching to say it. My tongue and lips are moving and drying out with how badly those words want to emerge. "You don't deserve sisters. Any of you," she says. She sounds like a snake. Hissing.

"What do you know about sisters? You don't even talk about yours! Astrid and Eleanor have no idea you ever had one! You forget all about her!" I say because I can't hold it in anymore. I throw my hand to lips, sticking the whole fist inside to shut myself up. I bite on the fingers, I can't believe what came out of my mouth. We don't talk about secrets. If Mom doesn't talk about her sister, it's because we're not allowed to bring her up. I know better.

Mom's hand raises into the air. It's going to come down on me. I curl into a ball on the stairs. I make a squealing pig sound I didn't even know was inside of me. But at the last minute Mom shifts her arm so that her hand crashes against the wall instead of me.

She falls to pieces.

Mom sits on the stairs and crumbles. She holds her own hand and cries. The house has never felt bigger or lonelier. I should do something, but I don't know what. I guess I sort of deserve this, from looking away when it happened to my sisters. We're all in it alone. I have to stay strong.

No part of me wants to touch her, but I stay next to her and look to make sure her hand's not bleeding or anything. For a minute, a really long one, I try to be Eleanor.

"We have to get her out of the closet," Mom weeps. It's muffled and I could be hearing her wrong, and I certainly don't want to ask any follow-up questions. "We have to get her unstuck."

My heart thumps. *The closet*, she said. Mom thinks

someone is stuck in the closet.

I'm caught between asking more questions and leaving her alone.

I'm weak and scared and not good enough to actually do anything useful, so I leave her on the stairs like that.

seventeen

I don't know where to go, so I go to the lake. Marla and Astrid are there. Eleanor must be with her secret boyfriend.

I don't tell them everything that happened. Just that Mom is upset with me and Dad is at work and I had to leave. And that I have an idea for my closet, whenever we think we can go back to the house.

I don't tell them that Mom basically said her sister, who we didn't even know about, is stuck in a closet. I'm scared if I say anything like that, Eleanor and Astrid will decide the closets are too evil, and they'll lock them all up. It's too sad to think about. We need the closets.

We watch the lake but don't swim.

Eleanor joins us later. We don't talk all afternoon.

When Eleanor stands up, we all follow. We're turning into zombies.

When we get close to the house, we slow down even more. We walk with straight legs and hunched backs and nervous fingers.

But when we go inside, it's empty. Mom's gone.

The place that Mom hit on the wall looks the same as the rest of the wall, but it seems like it should be marked. There should be a hole or a scratch or a warning sign. Mom didn't leave a note, but her car's gone, so we know she's traveled farther than down the street.

We stand in a circle in the hallway with no idea what to do, until I realize I know exactly what we should do.

"I've been thinking about one of Dad's fairy tales," I say. They'll think it's a strange and stupid thing to say. And I definitely hate the sound of my own voice: too high and too breathy and always sounding like a question instead of an answer. I'm doing this all wrong, as usual.

"Not you too," Marla says. She doesn't get Dad and his fairy tales and his studies and the way he tells stories instead of ever talking about real life.

"It's a fairy tale about closets," I say. "So I made it. In my closet." I'm not making sense, and Eleanor's getting all sweaty worrying about why Mom is gone, and it's not the right time. But I've said it and I can't take it back.

"You want to be in a fairy tale?" Astrid says. She tries to sound nice.

"Exactly!" I say, latching on even though she has no idea what I'm talking about. "There are these princesses, in this fairy tale, and I think maybe we're them. Or we're *like* them." I try to keep my voice calm. I try to lower the tone and make the words steady like a certainty instead of going up like a question.

Marla sighs.

"Not really them. But I think it would be fun. To try to make the fairy tale. It's all about sisters and closets and disappearing to a place no one can find you." This all made sense when I was in the basement finding plastic tiaras and half-dressed Barbies.

It's not making any sense now. Not even to me. Instead it's a sign that I'm being the desperate kind of Silly. The one who comes out when Mom's sick.

"Oh," Eleanor says.

"Okay!" Astrid says, though it sounds forced.

"I know how it sounds," I say. There's that breathiness back in my voice again.

"This is stupid. We need to find Mom," Marla says. "Why were you so mean to her?" She's glaring at me. "We don't have time for fairy tales right now, okay?"

"I thought you loved all the closets," I say. I'm careful to emphasize the word *all* so that she knows I could tell Astrid and Eleanor everything about her secret adventures in Astrid's bad closet. I don't like her high-and-mighty attitude.

"You don't care about Mom," Marla says like she always does. She clutches my arm on the word *Mom*, and I feel the squeeze in my stomach, in my heart, deep below my eyes.

"We all care about Mom," I say. "But she's not here right now, and we can do something cool in my closet." I give her a look to remind her she doesn't even have a closet that works, so her opinion doesn't matter too terribly much. It doesn't convince her of anything. She's fuming, but with Eleanor and Astrid agreeing to come inside, Marla's not about to be left out.

It's cramped with all four of us in my little closet. All four of us and the Barbies and shoes and tiaras and bowl of water and everything else I've gathered to re-create the fairy tale. Before I close the door, I make my sisters read the story out loud. No one seems very convinced by the similarities.

"Huh," Astrid says.

"Oh yeah," Eleanor says. "I remember this one."

Marla is refusing to speak.

When we close the door, things transform quickly. The bowl of water becomes the lake I had imagined. Trees grow from a few branches I'd laid on the ground. The silver and gold necklaces wrap themselves around the trees, over the walls, around each other. They go from dull to glittering, a quick burn, like they have caught flame.

The little plastic boat meant for the bathtub grows to fit the lake. It rocks with the small waves, and I climb on. Eleanor and Astrid can't stop looking at the gold and silver vines, which keep intensifying in sparkle. My sisters try to join me on the boat, but when they try to put their feet on the surface, they slide right off. It won't let them connect. The opposite of gravity.

I'm as frustrated as they are. I thought the closet was supposed to give me what I want. And I want them with me. I want them with me all the time. I'm about to say something, but I remember what Astrid actually said about the closets. That they will give me what I need, not what I want.

Like Astrid trying to climb the flower petals with me, some parts of my closet are only for me. Maybe I need that. Something of my own. The boat buzzes underneath me, changing and rumbling with magic from my touch.

"You think that boat's gonna bring you to a prince or something? That's what you want?" Marla says. She's grumpy, but at least she's finally speaking.

"No!" I say. I don't want any princes. I wasn't looking for a boy to dance with. I wasn't looking to dance at all. I only wanted to know if there's some other life we could be living. If in some other reality, we are princesses at a ball and not girls stuck in a house with a sick mom and a clueless dad.

Marla points at the line of Barbies I'd set up near the closet door. "Did you think they were going to turn into people? That they would become our sisters? This is so stupid. Let's go back into Eleanor's closet. Let's make a Rome diorama. You know Rome is Mom's favorite city?"

"I thought we could do better than regular boring cities," I say. "This is better."

The Barbies are still only plastic dolls with the pinkest lips and stiff joints and never-changing expressions. The closet did nothing for them. They didn't become princesses. They didn't turn into more sisters. They aren't dancing on the boat with me.

Maybe if I touched them they'd turn into real people, but I don't do it. I'm not sure I need any more sisters, now that I think about it. Maybe I'm the wrong one to have the special closet powers. I'm too scared and silly to do anything with them.

The shoes I brought inside aren't becoming worn, like the fairy tale, although they are dancing. In the air. Clacking their heels, stepping up and down the walls, tapping and balleting and making complicated patterns in the space above our heads. Astrid and Eleanor can't stop giggling at them. They are falling over themselves with delight. It doesn't matter how bad a mood Marla is in. I get to be proud of the way Astrid and Eleanor are smiling.

"What do you think happened after, with the princesses?" Marla says. "I mean, if you think there's some meaning there, then what happened next?" She won't give it up. The boat I'm on has found a perfect lazy rhythm. I want to let it put me to sleep. An UnWorry sleep, the kind I haven't had in way too long. I don't let the closet expand to a larger size. I want to stay in the boat near my sisters, not journey on the lake by myself.

"They lived happily ever after," I say. Marla's face shifts, and I guess I've given her an answer she likes. She'd never admit it, but she likes the world I've created too. At least a little bit.

"I feel some Happily Ever After feelings when I get out of the closets," Marla says. We're all thinking of that dreamy post-closet state, the transformation that I only wish we could hold on to.

"It's not Happily Ever After if it doesn't last," I say.

"For now, this is amazing," Eleanor says. "You're amazing. We're amazing!" She grabs my hands as I step off the boat and spins me around. It's dizzying. The dancing shoes come down to the ground, and Eleanor squeals. I'm not sure she's done that since she was much, much younger than me. She imitates the shoes, mimicking the steps they're making across the ground.

Then Eleanor and Astrid and I are dancing with the dancing shoes. And maybe we are not the Twelve Dancing Princesses, but by the time we are done, our feet are tired, the dancing shoes are worn and have broken heels, and I feel good and pretty and full.

Close enough.

eighteen

Dad's voice calling for us is the first thing we hear when we leave the closet and the sparkling lake and golden trees.

"Girls? Marla? Silly? El? Where are you all hiding?"

"We're here, Dad!" I push out of the room and into the hallway without checking to make sure I'm not covered in glitter or water or accidentally wearing dancing shoes. My much smarter sisters stay behind and clean themselves up before joining me.

"I got a call," he says. His voice has serious gravel in it, and his face is a wrong gray color. "Everything's fine," he says, even though it's definitely not. "But your mom had a little driving problem."

Marla starts groaning. She doesn't ask questions, she simply holds her head in her hands and groans.

"What does that mean?" Eleanor asks. She's sweating above her top lip and all over her collarbone. A slick sheen I'm dying to wipe off for her.

"She hit a tree," Dad says. His voice is shaking but he's got a smile on, and the effect is awful. It's impossible to guess how we should be acting, with him smiling and turning gray and rolling his cell phone between his hands like it's clay and not an electronic device. "Tapped it, really. Lightly."

Astrid takes a few steps away from the conversation, toward her room.

"It was a very small tree," Dad says.

I start laughing.

Not because it's funny. It is far from funny. But I'm still a little dizzy and loopy from the closet, and even I know there's something terribly wrong with that clarification.

"No one's hurt," he says. He doesn't seem to hear me laughing. I keep it under my breath, hold it in so hard I'm sure my face is turning red and my shoulders, then elbows, then hands are shaking. "These things happen."

"Where is she?" Eleanor says. Her hands are sweating too.

Dad takes a deep breath. So deep the floor below him creaks. This house is so old and strange it feels things with us.

"Can we come with you to get her?" Marla says when she's all out of groans.

"I'm sleepy," Astrid says, to no one in particular.

"She's with the police," Dad says. He speaks too low and too fast, the same way I do when I don't really want Marla to hear what I'm saying to her.

"The police came?" Eleanor wraps her hand around the back of her neck, where I assume the sweat is the worst. I'm so distracted by taking inventory of my sisters I forget to recognize how I'm doing. Am I okay? Am I still laughing? Am I crying? Is my heart beating or breaking?

I'm laughing. Still. The laughs are bigger now. Audible and undisguisable.

"Silly, stop it!" Marla says. She's crying and stomping her foot.

"The police came and got her. She was probably a little too, um, tired to be driving."

"Tired," Eleanor says.

"Your mom has had a really hard week," Dad says. Marla nods, but the rest of us don't respond at all. It doesn't sound true. And Dad smiles that awful, trying-too-hard smile again.

"I think Mom's really sick again," I say. I can't quite wring the laughter out of my voice entirely. But I try to sound serious. Everyone looks surprised I'm attempting to talk at all.

"She's doing much better since we got here," Dad says. "She went on a bike ride the other day! Didn't you hear?"

I wait for one of my sisters to jump in, but none of them does. They look at the carpet and at the rosebud wallpaper, and I wonder how different our lives would be if the walls were beige instead of flowered.

"LilyLee's mom goes to yoga every day and horseback riding with LilyLee every weekend and only ever sleeps at night," I say. "LilyLee's mom is taking her to Salem to see the witches, and they never have to move houses to help her feel better or anything." I think about the postcard I'm going to get from LilyLee's trip to Salem. Dad always said he'd take us there and tell us all the different witch stories in the world. He hasn't.

"Silly," he says, shaking his head and walking down the stairs, away from us. "You don't understand."

"Is it because of her sister?" I say. He comes back up. Eleanor looks confused. Marla mouths, *Shut up*. Dad clears his throat.

"I asked Mom not to talk about that," Dad says. He looks at each of us, to see what we know. Eleanor and Astrid know nothing, so their faces tense and twist. "There's no reason to know every sad thing in the world. And Mom doesn't quite remember what happened correctly."

"But where'd the sister go?" I say. "Mom says she's stuck."

Dad scratches his head like a gorilla. "She died, honey. A long, long time ago."

"Is that why Mom's so sad?" Marla asks, of course.

"What are you talking about?" Eleanor says. She's never been the last to know anything, so she's extra confused. "What sister?"

"You know how we've talked about ghost stories?" Dad says. He relaxes, figuring out a way to talk to us in his language. "Sometimes people are haunted. And ghosts aren't white things in sheets. They're the scary bits of the past that follow us around. You understand?"

Like this, I think. Like the way we'll all carry this summer around forever. The way we'll be haunted by Mom and her sickness and the twisty-turny way it unfolds.

"Mom's haunted?" Marla says. Dad shakes his head and shrugs and nods, all in a row. I don't know what it means.

Eleanor and Astrid probably have a billion questions, but no energy to ask them. And I'm pretty sure Dad's wrong about the sister being dead and that he doesn't know what I know—that Mom thinks her sister is caught in a closet.

Now that we know about the magic closets, I know anything is possible.

Then Dad's gone and Astrid's looking for crayons to put in her diorama and we're left waiting to see what happens next.

Not happily ever after at all.

I go to my room and they follow me. That has never happened before. I'm supposed to follow them.

I empty my closet of the "Twelve Dancing Princesses" experiment and decide I'm stupid for thinking there was anything to it.

"You're supposed to tell us everything you know," Eleanor says.

"I tried," I say.

"I wasn't sure," I say.

"Marla knew too," I say.

I don't say that I think Dad's wrong. That I think the mysterious sister is caught in a closet. That Mom has been searching for her for weeks.

"I'm sorry," I say, but Eleanor doesn't reply, and Astrid gives the weakest smile that ever was, and Marla pulls her knees to her chest and cries.

nineteen

I t's not long before I am desperate to go back into a closet. Being angry with Dad turns into being worried about Mom, and that turns into this gray-colored anxiety that replaces all the blood and air in me. Like I'm filled with cold, shivering sludge.

"Is your diorama done?" I ask Astrid. Her door is partially open, and she's cross-legged on the floor with glue and sunflower seeds and felt and pipe cleaners and this tiny turquoise elephant I'd forgotten we each had from Christmas stockings a few years ago.

"Not yet. We need an extra-good one," she says.

"I really didn't know anything about Mom's sister," I say.

"You know sometimes she says things, and she said it when she wasn't feeling well, and I thought maybe it wasn't—"

"Everything out here is so, so sad," Astrid says, cutting me off. "Maybe we don't need to know anything else about Mom and Mom's life and stuff. I'd rather play with the closets."

"Me too," I say, but it's not quite true, and if I can't be honest around Astrid, I can't be honest around anyone. "Sometimes."

I crane my neck to see if Eleanor's in there with Astrid, but she's not.

"Eleanor's getting ice cream?" I say. Astrid wipes something away from her eye—an eyelash? A tear? I can't tell—and nods. I should have guessed.

I picture Eleanor with a cup of chocolate chip and her not-that-cute, not-that-secret boyfriend, and I think I get it. It's like a closet too. Being in love is probably a place that's far away from this place—sweeter and more romantic and her own.

And I'd bet anything that for a time, being a twin was sort of like a closet too. A private kind of magic all their own. Maybe that's why Astrid and Eleanor don't seem as in tune with the closets as Marla and me. They don't need them as desperately.

"This diorama's going to be amazing," Astrid says. "Better than a vacation."

"Of course," I say. We're quiet for long enough to hear Marla still groaning in the next room. "Hurry up with it, okay?"

I think we both know how quickly everything's changing. A little bit more shifts every day. Every day Eleanor stays with her secret boyfriend a few minutes longer and Mom does something a little stranger and Marla gets a little grumpier.

Another thing I think might be true: every day Marla's wrist turns a new color. Every day she adds another bangle to her pile of bracelets. Things we've won at arcades and carnivals and gotten as treats in goody bags and bought at the mall and gotten as stocking stuffers. Bracelets I've never seen her wear before.

"I'm scared," I say. It feels good to hear it out loud.

"We won't lose Eleanor," Astrid says. "That guy's not half as cute as Henry."

I don't know how to say I'm more scared of losing Mom. I leave Astrid so that she can perfect our next diorama, and I wander the house looking for solutions.

There's a pile of fabric in the sewing room, next to the sewing machine. I go through all of it, and find something dark blue and velvety. I think it was going to be for Astrid's wizard costume last Halloween, but Mom was really sick in the fall, so she didn't make costumes for any of us. We had to get store-bought.

I don't know why the fabric is out here now, but I know it's not because Mom was getting a head start on this year's costumes.

The fabric is amazing, and Astrid would have loved it slung over her back for Halloween, but I can use it for something even better now. There are yards upon yards of it, and I lug it all to my closet. I hang it from the bar and the hooks and place it on the ground. The closet is darker and softer by the time I'm done.

I look around my room for more things to add. I stick plain metal and yellow and purple thumbtacks into the velvet. I have a mobile of the planets and an inflatable globe that I bring inside. Dad has this Astroturf he uses to practice his golf game indoors: a strip of fake green grass, and I sneak into his office to borrow that too. It fits pretty well. For good measure I throw pink pipe cleaners onto the fake grass and twist a few of them around the clothing rod above my head.

It doesn't look pretty. It looks the way a lot of my craft projects look. I don't have Astrid's skill at making the ordinary look extraordinary. I don't have her eye for detail. I don't glue things with care. I almost don't want to close the closet door. I don't want to feel the sink of disappointment at my sloppiness. I don't want it to be confirmed how messy and uncoordinated I am. How badly I need my sister's supervision.

I should wait for Astrid to make a perfect diorama, but I need to feel okay now. I can't wait.

I step inside. The door clicks shut and I squeeze my eyes. Squeeze myself.

When minutes have passed and I can't stand the suspense any longer, I let my eyes open.

It's night in the closet. It's a velvety, navy-blue night.

I trip, even though I was standing still.

The thumbtacks have been transformed into stars. Some are gold, the color stars are supposed to be. But the others are neon yellow or purple and glowing, alien-like and strange against the surface of the night I created. The pipe cleaners have turned to vines that wrap around themselves and the rod, which somehow still stretches over my head, but now into infinity, since the walls have vanished and been swallowed up by the night. More pink vines worm their way over the ground, which is a fluorescent green, but instead of being fake plastic turf, it is actively growing at the pace of a centimeter a minute.

It is beautiful.

Not only beautiful—strange. It is everything I placed inside the closet, but better. Weirder. Alive.

I lie on the ground and look up at the stars I have created. When I was little, Astrid and I used to talk about rearranging the stars in the night sky to make our own constellations. I have done exactly that now.

The closet stops feeling like a closet. It is timeless, placeless space. The grass tickles my arms as it grows at its ridiculous rate. Soon, if I look to my left or right, I can barely see above the growth. That doesn't matter, as long as I can look up at the stars.

When Mom was doing well, she asked me once what I like so much about the stars. I wasn't sure. "The sparkle?" I said, but that wasn't right. "That there are so many? Or that they are all there but sometimes you can't see them, but when you can see them, they're the best?" Mom nodded along with all of it. She used to be a good listener.

"They don't really sparkle," she said after a while. I was squinting my eyes to better see the shapes they made in the sky. It was working. "They glow. It's warmer, sweeter, deeper than a sparkle. They glow, and make things seem unending and okay."

"They glow," I said.

"How bad can it be in a world where you only have to wait until night to see the sky glowing, telling you warmth can always, always poke through?" She sighed after she spoke, and I thought that was it, that was the moment when Mom would shift from sad to happy, from sleepy to awake.

~

I want to hold a star.

One star in particular seems to glow in my direction.

I'm warm and golden feeling.

I could never feel this way without the magic, without the help of the closet and the stars and the night sky I made myself.

I could never feel this way in any other part of the house.

I reach up on my tiptoes and grab at the night I created. Something warm hits my palm, and I close my hand around it and pull down. The star dislodges from the sky without much trouble. It has a bit of a heartbeat. An unusual thump of heat in my hand.

I am holding a star.

I keep thinking about the sad, lost way my sisters and I have been wandering around the house and the road to the lake, and the takeout dinners Dad thinks we like ordering and the piles of fabric in Mom's sewing room that never get turned into anything.

I think about Mom at the police station and Dad using all his energy to smile and Eleanor choosing to spend Christmas and New Year's and spring break and Sunday mornings with her secret boyfriend instead of us. I think about Marla.

I think about Mom's sister.

And it's all so sad that it feels like I won't be able to handle it. Like I won't be able to leave the closet and face the real world.

So I do what I'm certain the closet wants me to do. What I'm allowed to do but my sisters can't. I take that little star with me.

Only yesterday, Marla was completely unable to take a tiny handful of dirt out of the closet, but something inside me tells me I can steal something magical from this sky.

Maybe it's my sisters telling me I'm special, or maybe it's some twin-like bond I have with the closet, but I know how badly I want to take something with me into the real world, and I feel sure the closet will let me.

Because the closet gives you what you need, and I'm special, when it comes to closets, and I need this.

The star buzzes in my hand, and I decide that is confirmation that this is what I'm supposed to do.

The rest of the fantasy night fades away when I head back into my bedroom, but I manage to hang on to the star. It doesn't fade with the rest of the magic.

My sweaty hand is strangling its glowing heat. When I look at it in the bright light of my bedroom, it's even more startling: pointed and throbbing and a golden-orange color that I have never seen before. Sunset Nectarine. Pumpkin Marigold Moon. Autumn Candlelight.

Maybe when I grow up I'll be in charge of naming new Crayola colors.

I put it in my jewelry box. It's smaller than the palm of my hand, the size of a half-dollar, which Eleanor used to collect. I don't think the jewelry box is the best place for it. But I'm not sure there are any rules for where to put a stolen star.

I think at least it will help me sleep, and it's about time to sleep now. I don't know how it came to be night, but the thing about watching the stars is that you can watch for three minutes or three hours and it feels exactly the same.

twenty

In the very early morning I think I can hear the star. A pretty buzzing noise, like a mosquito who has mastered the violin.

I check on it, in its box. It glows, winking warmth at me.

I hear something else too. Astrid and Eleanor's door opening and clicking closed. Slippered feet tiptoeing. Marla's door opening and closing.

Because of our lifetime of summers spent in this house, I know the sounds of the doors perfectly. Like being able to tell the difference between Mom's footsteps and Eleanor's, I know from the squeak and click which door is being opened and who is doing the opening.

I leave my room and wonder if my sisters have the same door-sense that I do. They must, because Marla opens her door before I reach it. Her hair is wild and her eyes are black. I step inside her room.

"You went back in," I say. Marla's lips are almost purple. Her skin has lost all the color it had been building from our time on the beach and is nearly translucent. "You look awful."

"Everything's okay," Marla says. Her voice is an unusual register, low and new, like she has a cold. "I'm great. You should go in. You need it. You need to go into Astrid's closet." She takes a step or two toward me, and even the way she's walking doesn't seem familiar. Her hand touches my elbow, and it's ice.

"What did you see in there?" I say. I think there are tiny cuts on her hands and forearms. I look at her feet, and they look hurt too.

"Roses," Marla says. But they obviously aren't the roses from Astrid's dioramas. They aren't the pretty grass-growing roses we saw in Eleanor's closet. They aren't even the dehydrated rosebushes from our Massachusetts backyard.

"And thorns?" I say, reaching my forefinger to the torn palm of her hand.

"I guess."

"What else?"

"Only the roses," Marla says, like she's recalling the best dream she's ever had. The best dream anyone's ever had. "Black roses covering every inch of the closet. Can you think of anything more beautiful? I was so sad, and that's what it made for me. I'm going back in, but I wanted to grab a pair of scissors, so I can try to take some of the roses out."

I don't like the idea of scissors in Astrid's closet. I don't like the idea of Marla in there at all, but especially not with sharp objects that could grow larger and sharper.

Scissors with a mind of their own. I can't think of anything worse.

I know Marla won't be able to take anything out of that closet. And Marla knows she wasn't able to get anything out of Eleanor's closet.

I could help her, I guess. But I won't.

"I'll go in with you later if you make breakfast with me now," I say. It's a lie—I have no intention of ever going in that closet again—but I need to distract her. "We can make something special for Mom."

Marla lights up. She doesn't snap out of her strange state, but she smiles a more familiar smile.

"She really needs something special," Marla says. "She's

had such a hard few weeks. I was going to bring her one of the roses, but maybe breakfast is better. She'd love breakfast, I bet."

It sounds like the kind of thing Dad says when he's pretending Mom's not super sick. My stomach lurches, and I don't know if it makes me a bad daughter, but I would never, ever give my star to Mom. It's all mine.

We head to the kitchen and I help Marla make pancakes. There's a basket of freshly picked blueberries on the counter. Probably Eleanor went blueberry picking yesterday with her secret boyfriend. It's exactly the kind of annoyingly romantic activity I'm sure they're constantly doing. I throw some of the blueberries into the batter.

Marla does the bacon. She knows how to burn it for Mom and doesn't mind the fiery-hot oil that spits off the pan when it's frying.

Marla flips the pancakes and I know they won't taste as good as if Eleanor or Dad made them.

Eleanor and Astrid come down, still half asleep but smelling bacon and blueberries and butter.

Astrid sits on the counter and eats berries straight from the basket.

Neither of them says anything about the scratches all over Marla's hands and feet and arms, but Marla throws on Mom's old gray sweatshirt, which was folded over one of the stools.

It's strange on her—too big in most places and smelling all wrong for a girl our age. I almost ask her to take it off. We all have to work hard to be less like Mom, not more like her.

"I didn't say you could have those berries," Eleanor says. "I was going to make muffins for—for my friend." She still won't say his name. Which is probably safest. And fine by me. I don't need to know it. Astrid used to make handmade cards and woven leather bracelets for Henry. When Mom found out about them, she took away all of Astrid's leather strings and the rubber stamps she used to make the cards.

"You can't do that," I say. I don't want to know what Mom would do if she found out about this secret boyfriend. We don't need any more Big Events, that's for sure. We need to keep things calm and have all our adventures in the safety of my and Eleanor's closets.

"We thought Mom could use a nice breakfast," Marla says. I roll my eyes. I am really becoming awful.

"I didn't pick those for Mom," Eleanor says. She has that pre-crying look—pink, watery eyes, but not actually letting the tears out.

"Mom's not here," Dad says. We hadn't heard him come down.

"Did she go for a run?" I say. I sound too excited. When Mom's going on morning runs, it means she's on the road to recovery.

"No. She's Away," Dad says. We hear the capital *A* of the word, even if we can't see it when he speaks.

It's quiet, aside from the popping sound of bacon frying and the creaking house.

"Where?" Eleanor asks. Her forehead shines. She looks like she can't decide whether she's happy or sad.

"Arizona," Dad says. "For one month at least."

"But why?" Marla says. Astrid starts humming a song that's been on the radio a lot.

"The police said she has to," Dad says. He doesn't say that he thinks she needs to, also. "I don't want you worrying about this, though. Everything's fine." He coughs, like that will erase what he said.

"We made pancakes," I say, when no one speaks.

"I can see that," Dad says. He doesn't make a move to serve himself or us. I pile more pancakes off the pan and onto a plate and think how sad it will be if they go to waste.

I don't think about Mom or what Dad's saying about police and stuff. I want to take the blueberries into the closet and watch them glow or grow or turn into a lake of blueberry juice.

Astrid slips out to the porch, and Marla stomps up to her room.

"She didn't say good-bye!" Marla yells on her way up the stairs.

I get the syrup and a few pancakes and dig in.

Eleanor and Dad do too.

"I'm sorry," Dad says, but I don't know for what. There are so many things.

twenty-one

I hear from Mom first. A postcard comes in the mail four days later. The image is of brown land and a green cactus and a bunny with ears that stand up straight instead of flopping. It says ARIZONA! in big red block letters. The exclamation point seems especially cruel.

So many bunnies here! Mom writes. *I know you love postcards. And I love you. I'll be home soon.*

Mom hasn't said I love you to anyone in months.

Instead of writing Mom back, I write a postcard to LilyLee. I tell her my mom is Away again, and that I wish

I could come over to her house. I know LilyLee will think it's cool that I'll get more postcards from Arizona. But I've never been very interested in Arizona.

"You get a postcard from Mom and don't even write her back," Marla says. "It's not fair."

twenty-two

Dad gets a letter a few days later. He reads it in his room and doesn't come out for the rest of the night, so we get to order pizza and watch an R-rated movie on TV.

"When's Mom going to write me?" Marla asks when the movie's over and the pizza's gone. She seems extra-aggravated, so I know she hasn't been in any closets. We've all been staying out of them. I don't know why, except it's hard to do much of anything the first few days Mom's gone. It's too strange. We mostly sleep and watch TV that we're not really even watching.

But I've been holding my star for a few minutes a few times a day. The warmth from it travels through my whole body, and I love the almost unhearable buzz it makes all night long.

twenty-three

Next Mom sends a package for Astrid and Eleanor.

"No," Marla says when she sees it on the counter. We're lake-wet and frizzy-haired from a morning spent splashing in the water, and we're tracking footprints into the kitchen because Dad's too out of it to tell us what to do.

"A package came for the twins!" Dad says, oblivious.

"We're not one person," Eleanor says, when she sees the address written out in Mom's messy handwriting. Eleanor's in her new bikini, with nothing but a pair of tiny jean shorts over it. The bikini is red and ridiculous and obviously for her secret boyfriend. "You open it," she says to Astrid.

Astrid's hair is dripping onto her legs and the floor, and

she looks more like a mermaid than a person. I hope I look that way too.

"No, thank you," Astrid says. We stand over the package and watch it. It does nothing, of course. It's a package, not an animal.

"What about me?" Marla says. There is nothing on the kitchen counter for her.

"I'm sure you're next!" Dad says. He is guzzling coffee and says he wishes he could take the day off to *hang out*. He thinks this is a very cool turn of phrase that will make us think he is a friend and not a dad, but he's got on his long jean shorts and "Don't Take New Hampshire for Granite" sweatshirt, which is some extremely sad joke, and a Mets cap that looks too new to be cool. When he wears that hat, people ask him if he's from New York. He's not.

He says he's not really from anywhere. When he's asked about it, he launches into some story about wandering men without homes and the classic trope of orphan stories and the difference between stories set in specific places versus those set in vague settings. Conversations with Dad always turn into academic discussions, never into personal talks.

When we were little, Mom used to say he rode in on a white horse, like a prince. We believed her for a while. He looks like he could be a prince. Or a duke, at least.

"Why am I last?" Marla says. Dad takes hot chocolate

off the shelf and grabs five mugs and a carton of milk and starts mixing and heating. It's not exactly a summer drink, and none of us actually want hot chocolate right now, but at least he's sort of trying to take care of us, so no one complains.

"Save the best for last!" Dad says, which is actually insulting to the rest of us, but we don't get prickly about it, because we're used to this kind of comment being thrown around to make Marla happy.

"I wrote her a letter and asked her *questions*," Marla says. "I sent her a drawing of me and her hiking in Arizona together. It took me all afternoon."

"She hasn't been there that long yet," Dad says. "Maybe she didn't get your letter yet."

"Why don't you open the package, Marla?" Astrid says, watching her like she's a thing that might explode. "I'm sure it's for all of us." Marla shakes her head, and we watch the milk for a few moments in silence. When it's done, Dad puts a steaming mug of cocoa in front of each of us. Marla doesn't take a sip.

"She probably assumes we're all sharing everything," Eleanor says. "And we are! Everything! Of course!" It's too much. My ears hurt from the screeching enthusiasm.

"Can you please open it so we can all move on?" Marla says at last. Dad moves behind Marla and rubs her shoulders, but she shrugs him off, her eyes not moving from the package on the counter. He doesn't seem to know what else to do to help the moment be less awful, so he heads out to the porch.

"Let me know if you need anything," he says. We need so, so much.

Astrid dives in. She opens the package with the finesse of a small puppy. She tears at corners where there is thick tape, ignores the "Open Here" arrow, and turns a perfectly square box into a pile of cardboard. There's an envelope on top, and Eleanor picks that up. She reads out loud,

> *"Astrid and El:*
>
> *Some souvenirs from Arizona!*
>
> *It is nice here. Calm and sort of quiet, but the good kind. I miss you terribly and promise I will be home in time to compete in the Sand Castle Contest with you.*
>
> *When you go to the lake, watch your sisters. Marla isn't very good in the water, and Silly is reckless. You know that already, of course, but I'm a mother, and mothers remind you to do things.*
>
> *I'm still your mother.*
>
> *In one year or five we'll all remember this as a good summer, one that mattered.*
>
> *Be good. Especially you, Eleanor.*
>
> *Love, Mom."*

Neither Eleanor nor Astrid goes through the rest of the box.

"You can have it," Eleanor says, handing the whole thing over to Marla.

"I'm tired," Astrid says. They both disappear into their room. I'd follow them, but Marla is going through the objects very carefully, and when Marla's careful, it makes me nervous.

In the package Marla finds more bracelets, which she immediately slips onto both wrists. There's also a book called *The Roles We Play*, which, according to the picture on the front, is about sad siblings and sadder parents, so I guess we're not the only ones. There are a couple of Arizona pens and a bug encased in amber and some stones that look historical instead of pretty.

"I'm keeping it all," Marla says.

I don't want to think too hard about Mom packing all the objects into the box, or whether she thinks they're enough to make up for everything else.

Marla's so engrossed she probably won't even notice. She's the only one who wants to see the objects, and she's the only one who hasn't actually gotten anything in the mail.

I don't really want to think too hard about that particular sadness either. If we were the siblings on the front of the book Mom sent, Marla would be the one tugging on the mother's shirt while the mother looks away.

I head back to my room and check on my star, let the warmth hit my face. It calms me down a little, but I need more. So I grab a few art supplies I've been hoarding from the cabinet downstairs and head into the closet. I'm ready to go back. I'm ready to snap out of the Mom-daze.

Within moments, I'm lying on a beach of pink crystallized sand, and there is an ocean made of blue feathers lapping at my feet. It should be a dream. It has all the signs of a dream: hyperactive colors and never-before-seen landscaping and the way I feel calm and light. I feel my UnWorry.

I'm laughing at the way the feathers tickle my toes when there's a knock at my door.

"Hm?" I say. I can't muster up words. I'm not ready to leave this moment, this place I created with nothing more than a handful of plastic beads and a bag of feathers that Dad bought when Astrid insisted she wanted to be a bluebird for Halloween.

"I need you," Marla says from the other side of the closet door. She isn't whining, which is sort of unlike her lately. I roll onto my stomach and reach my fingertips toward the waves of feathers. I'm not ready to leave. Marla knocks again. "Silly. Get out of there."

"Give me a little bit," I say. I dig my hands into the sandy crystals, then lift them up again. I could do that same movement over and over all day and I don't think it would get old.

Marla swings the door open. I jump up and take a step outside the closet. The beach of feathers and crystals is mine, and I'm not ready to share it with Marla.

Quickly, the feathers turn all fake and cheap, and the sand is a pile of plastic beads that are now cracked and broken, and the light is ugly and the closet smells like feet and the world I created is officially completely gone.

Marla hugs me. It's not like we've never hugged before, but we don't do it often, that's for sure. Her body is skinnier than mine, bonier, all pointy and arrowed, and unexpected. Looking at her is so different from holding her.

I wonder if I'll grow straight and narrow like her. I'm not sure I'd want to be so bony. There aren't any soft parts of her, and I think it'd be scary to walk around the world without a bit of padding. She's so angular. The angles are how you get hurt, I think.

"Let's go," she says. We're still hugging, and it's impossible to talk and hug at the same time, as far as I'm concerned. I take a step back and wait for her arms to loosen, which they eventually do, but after way more time than any sort of normal hug.

"Go where?" I say. "And why?"

"I think if I show you more about Astrid's closet, you'll

get it," she says. "It's not evil. It's maybe a little scary some-times but in a good way." I shrug. "And I have an idea," she adds.

I shiver, thinking of the little dollop of Astrid's closet that I have already experienced. The way beautiful turned scary. The rapid speed of the wings flapping. The darkness in Marla's eyes. I don't want to experience any of that again.

"I need someone to help me," Marla says. "I need you."

"I'm good with my closet," I say as nicely as possible, because Marla looks like she really does need someone's help. But I'm mostly wondering if I can get Marla out of my room quickly so I can go back in the closet and re-create the world I had going. My hand finds the closet doorknob, grips it tightly.

Marla notices but doesn't make a move toward leav-ing. We're both quiet and still, each waiting for the other to move. Our house creaks and it makes me jump, but not Marla. Marla is steady.

"I did your thing for you," she says. "With the princesses and the boat and stuff. We tried that. Can't we try this? You and me?" There are rings under her eyes. Like she hasn't slept in forever. She looks more and more like Mom every day. I don't bother reminding her how very, very little she invested when we tried to make my fairy tale happen in the closet. She's right. She did, technically, do it for me.

"Maybe you should go in with Astrid. Since it's her closet? Don't you think?"

Marla is playing with things on my dresser: a tube of lip gloss, a fringed lampshade, a glass hippo figurine from when I thought I was maybe going to start collecting hippos. Her fingers find the jewelry box with the star inside. I hadn't thought to hide it. No one ever comes into my room.

"I don't want to go with Astrid," she says. Her fingers rub the velvety top of the box. My shoulders rise to my ears. She cannot open that box. "You know you're the special one. We all saw what you can do in there, how you're in control of them. Come on, Silly. I mean, Priscilla. Mom's always said you're the special one, and that we have to protect you and make sure you're okay and love you most of all. Maybe there's a reason?"

"No!" I yell. I leap toward Marla and the jewelry box and the star I'm hiding inside it. Marla jumps and fumbles with the box. It shakes and threatens to fall to the floor, but I grab it from her hands. "You can't come in here and touch all my things," I say. Marla's eyebrows rise up toward her hairline, to her crooked middle part, and she's either smirking or smiling, I can't tell for sure.

"Then let's get out of your room," she says.

I agree. Not because I think it's a good idea to go in Astrid's closet. But because I cannot let Marla see that star.

Astrid and Eleanor take an afternoon nap. It seems impossible. I can't imagine sleeping, maybe ever again. Marla knows the exact places to step on the usually creaky floor so that it doesn't creak. She knows how to turn the closet's doorknob without a sound, and how to breathe in time with Eleanor and Astrid's deep sleeping breaths so that they can't sense us in the room and wake up.

I'm scared of how often this means she's been in here.

She's already brought things into the closet. Leaves are stored in one corner. She's brought in orange construction paper and black toothpicks, and a few of Mom's old costume rings.

And as I should have guessed, everything from Mom's package. The bug and the stones and the pens and bracelets.

I spot the photo album that Mom was looking at. The one with pictures of her gone sister. I don't want to be in the closet with that. I don't like the collection, and I open my mouth to tell Marla as much, but she puts a finger to her lips and shakes her head. The closet door is still open. If we want to talk, we'll have to close the door and see what happens. I'm still convinced that if we tell Eleanor and Astrid about this closet, they'll find a way to lock up all the closets, and no matter how scared I am of the bad closet, I'm even more scared of losing my wonderful closet.

I have never wanted to leave a place more, but Marla hangs on to my elbow, her fingernails pressing into my skin. The twins breathe and shift in their sleep, and before I have a chance to sneak back out, Marla shuts the closet door with a muffled *click*.

We are stuck in the bad closet.

—❧

The leaves go black.

Black and sheer and veiny and then so, so big. They float up a few inches above our heads and hover there, like they may choose to suffocate us.

It starts to rain.

Marla's smiling. I always forget about the tiny dimple that dips into her skin right next to her lips when she grins. I forget how straight her teeth are, and how she is maybe the prettiest sister, when she is not being the meanest sister. Even with circles under her eyes and a strange stringiness to her hair, she is pretty. Healthy-Mom pretty.

"I caught Mom in here a few days before she left. Looking for something. I think if we find out what she's looking for, she'll be okay," Marla says.

"She thinks her sister's in here," I say. I don't mean to agree with Marla, but I'm so distracted by thoughts of the sister and what is true that it comes out.

"Then we'll find the sister," Marla says. Her eyes are wide, and she's bouncing on her toes. It makes me motion sick.

The walls are rotten-pumpkin orange. I have a headache.

"I bet Mom sent this all on purpose! So we'd bring it in here! She totally knows!" Marla pulls at my elbow. I'm already paying attention, but she wants more. "It's like a scavenger hunt! We have all the clues. I'm so positive. This will work. We'll figure it out."

I'm impossibly tired of hearing Marla talk about Mom.

"What if Mom doesn't know anything? What if Mom doesn't want to get better? What if the closets caused all the problems? What if there aren't any solutions?" I'm yelling even though we are supposed to be staying quiet. It feels so sweet, to feel my throat strain and to hear my own voice filling up the closet.

"Watch!" Marla says. She leans over the Arizona pens and the bug in amber, which she's put in the same corner of the room.

It doesn't take long.

The pen leaps up. It triples in size. The bug breaks out of the amber and grows too. It grabs the pen—it's a bug who knows how to draw, and I'm shaking and covering my eyes.

The bug starts drawing all over the closet walls. It draws

in the air too. Floating designs that aren't against any surface, but instead simply exist in the air around us. I swear one brushes against my ear, and I yip.

I work hard to not look at the bug's legs. There are so many, and they're thick and black and awful. Marla hates bugs usually. But right now she's grinning.

"Calm down. It feels good," Marla says. A squiggly line drawing wraps itself around her, like a snake. She giggles, as if the floating drawing feels more like a hug than a threat, but I don't buy it.

The rain hits harder. It pinches my skin and leaves little marks. For a moment there is a red bruise everywhere a raindrop has hit. I watch my skin as it polka-dots itself with pain, fades, and polka-dots itself again.

"I'm going to be sick," I say. I want to reach for Marla's hand, but I don't want to risk the squiggly black line wiggling itself around me. I don't want to touch it. The drawings that have hit my ears and the top of my head were hotter than I'd have expected.

The bug is all kinds of creepy and crawly. I'm going to cry, but I can't get a big enough breath to get a sob out.

"I hate it in here," I say. Marla dances in the rain. I can tell she is in charge of this closet, even if it's Astrid's.

If Astrid's right, that this closet takes on our feelings,

then of course Marla has control. Her feelings are the darkest and scariest and biggest. Hers are the most on the surface. Her feelings are the kind that scare me.

"Make it stop," I say. In my closet, I have control over the elements, and I look to Marla for reassurance that she has some kind of control in here. She shrugs. "Make it STOP," I say. I'm screeching now. I'm not even scared of Eleanor and Astrid hearing us. I can't see the closet door through all the chaos, and I wonder if Marla knows where it is. If she can get us out. If she ever will.

"Which part?" she says. Her voice is light, airy, Astrid-like. Not Marla-like at all. She's smiling at the phantom scribbles, the still-growing bug, reaching her fingertips out to touch them.

Once when Mom let me stay home from school, we watched a hypnotist on TV. I wasn't really sick, and she knew it. She said sometimes we all need days to stay in our pajamas and watch TV and not worry about anything other than what will make us happy in that moment. She stayed in her robe too. It was before she stayed in her robe all the time. We ate cheese and crackers. She drank a big glass of jewel-colored red wine, and she let me have four glasses of chocolate milk, even after it dribbled down my chin and onto the couch pillows.

The hypnotist talked in a low, monotonous voice and convinced audience members that they were roosters and made them dance every time someone sang "Happy Birthday." The way Marla is acting reminds me of those hypnotized audience members. Same wide eyes. Same slow movements. Same ability to be one person one moment, and another person the next.

I snap my fingers. That's what the hypnotist did to snap his subjects out of their trances.

It doesn't work. Marla still has a funny smile on her face, and she hasn't blinked in several long minutes.

The pen in the air writes words, finally, but not any I recognize. It writes the name *LAUREL* over and over and over. I don't know anyone named Laurel. I don't know that I even like the name Laurel.

"Who's Laurel?" I say. "Why is it doing that? Does it mean something? Are we supposed to do something?" I know I am asking too many questions and not leaving any room for Marla to answer them.

"You should really breathe," Marla says as an answer.

I see the door through a patch of not-written-on space, like a bit of fog has cleared, and I rush for it.

"Sometimes it sticks," she says. I pull and she's right. The door is sticking.

"You do it," I say, stepping away. I still feel like Marla is in charge of everything in here, from the writing to the creepy dark-orange color to the black leaves with black veins floating around us and starting to pile below my feet. I am wishing I had worn shoes, or slippers at least, because even the crunch of the leaves under my toes hurts a little more than it should. Not as badly as glass might, but sharper than leaves usually are.

"No thanks," Marla says. She sits in a pile of leaves, covering her feet with them, the way we sometimes cover our feet in sand at the beach. "I like the name Laurel, don't you?" she says. I pull at the closet door again. It feels like it might give in to me, but pulling hard doesn't seem to help.

"Marla. We have to get out! We can't stay in here!"

"Mom liked the name Laurel," Marla says. "She told me once."

"Just, like, randomly mentioned liking that name?" I breathe and hold the doorknob and try to open it with my mind, without pulling or pushing or turning anything. There's wind in the closet, and the rain is rushing down harder and faster. My wet hair keeps blowing into my eyes. The wind is picking up the now-wet leaves and throwing them around us.

"Put it together, Silly," Marla says. "I bet Laurel is her

sister. I really, really bet it is." She gets up and bounces on her toes again, parts of her all dark from the closet and other parts of her lit up with excitement. "We have to get Laurel, that's what it's telling us. We have to go save her. Bring her to Mom. Then Mom will be fine."

The pen writes *LAUREL* even more ecstatically, so Marla might be right, but if Laurel is Mom's lost sister, it could also be a warning that we will end up like her: stuck, like Mom obviously thinks Laurel is.

I don't know that the closets have things they want us to do. They're only supposed to give us what we need. And the bad closet is giving Marla what she needs—hope that she can save Mom.

The wind almost knocks me over.

"I don't care about Mom, we need to get out!" I say. The light dims even more; we are entirely in shade and shadows.

Marla gives me a long look. I can't quite decipher it.

"You're not scared," I say. Any normal person should be scared. I beg the door to open. Marla sighs and shrugs. I twist the knob and it pops open, like it was never stuck at all. I hadn't realized my heart was captured in my throat until the door opening released it and dropped it down to my toes. The feeling of a roller coaster as it rises and then drops too quickly, all of a sudden. Fear.

"Let's go," I say, reaching to grab Marla's hand but

changing my mind. I don't want to touch her. She doesn't look like my whiny, sometimes mean, always disgruntled, smallest big sister. She looks like someone else. Someone I don't want to be near.

twenty-four

Eleanor's night-light is on, and I can see that Marla's face is wet.

Her face is wet and her Mets T-shirt is ripped and her lips are so dry they are cracking. They are rocky deserts.

I am trying to keep us quiet, so we can sneak back out of Astrid and Eleanor's bedroom, but Marla is moaning. Quiet moans, but loud enough to interrupt the flow of sleeping breaths.

"Mmmm?" Eleanor hums out into the dark.

"Mmmm," Astrid responds.

"Ughhhh," Marla groans back.

"Shhhh," I say. I cover Marla's mouth with my hand,

but she's already lying down, finally out of the closet, and curling over her own stomach, circling her ribs with her arms like she may puke.

"Let me back in," Marla groans again, more loudly. "I have to go back in. I came out too soon."

I don't feel that way. When I leave my closet or Eleanor's, I have the UnWorry. I feel new. But exiting Astrid's closet, I mostly feel tired. And nervous. And then even more tired from how nervous I am. And above all else, relieved to be out.

"Mmmmm," Eleanor calls out, and this time I hear her body shift around on the bed, the squeaking springs, and I swear even the flutter of her eyelashes as she shifts from asleep to a little bit awake.

"Come on, get up," I whisper in Marla's ear, but she's not going anywhere, and I guess neither am I.

"Marla?" Astrid says. It seems impossible, how dark their room is in the afternoon with the shades pulled down. It makes me even more lonely for our old house, where the curtains always let at least a little light in. Marla doesn't answer, but I note that Astrid called her name and not mine, which makes me think that Astrid knows Marla has been sneaking in here from time to time. That maybe I haven't been carrying this secret all on my own after all.

"I'm here too," I say, keeping my voice low in the tiny

hope that Eleanor will fall back asleep.

"Silly? Who's in here? Is Mom okay? Where's Dad?" Eleanor says, popping up in bed and scrambling for the lamp.

"Mom's fine, I assume. Dad's in his room," I say.

"Marla?" Astrid says, and Marla moans in response. "*LIGHT*, Eleanor! My God, it's not like it's hard to find!" Astrid rarely gets mad, but when she does, it is sudden and certain.

"I'm not even totally awake!" Eleanor says. A few things drop on the floor, miniature crashes. She is obviously swatting her arm around, searching unsuccessfully for the switch, and when she finds it we are all shocked into the light and can all see just how terrible Marla really does look, hugging herself on the floor.

"You aren't okay," Eleanor says. She's sleepy from her nap, so her voice sounds like some combination of cat and frog and horse.

"I think it's food poisoning or something. I mean, otherwise I'm great," Marla says. Her eyes are dark again: navy blue instead of pale blue. She looks more like Mom than ever, with her ringed eyes and chapped lips and messy clothes.

And her frown.

"It's not food poisoning," Eleanor says. They must have noticed our wet clothes and strange expressions and the open door to the closet. The twins have been set into motion. Eleanor turns on more lights, closes the door to Astrid's closet, grabs her cup of water to give to Marla. Astrid goes to Marla's side to feel her forehead and lift her from lying down to sitting up. I mostly wring my hands and worry.

I don't need to be worrying. Eleanor has done exactly this before, taking care of Mom. She and Astrid have a routine down. Eleanor calls out commands, and Astrid follows them in a calm, focused way. They seem more comfortable now than I've ever seen them. Like this is what they do best.

"I'll go back in the closet," Marla says between whimpers. "I feel fine in there. It's better for me." Luckily, she's too tired to actually move. Astrid keeps a hand on Marla's forehead and another on her knee, and that's basically enough to keep her still for a good long while.

Eleanor sits down next to the rest of us when she has finished all the little chores around the room: blanket straightening and hair brushing and Advil getting. "We told you not to—"

"You were wrong!" Marla says. "It's a good closet. It's telling me what to do. It cares. You guys don't understand. But you will. You'll see."

Marla is smiling. It's a warm, lit-up smile, one I've maybe never seen on her face. Nothing like bitterness or sadness or rage behind it.

"Look in the mirror," Eleanor says. "You do not look okay. You need to see yourself. You're not seeing what we're seeing, okay, honey?" Eleanor has a handheld mirror, a silver thing that is heavy and engraved and beautiful, like from a fairy tale. But it's not so useful in terms of actually being able to see your reflection. It was passed down to her from Dad, who said it was from his family. I wonder who his family might have been, that they'd have something so magically beautiful. The glass is old and spotty and yellowed. Eleanor picks it up and shoves it in Marla's face. Marla shakes her head in a polite kind of *no, thank you*, and she pushes the mirror away.

"Let me back in," Marla says, keeping very still.

Astrid gets up and heaves Marla over her shoulder with a grunt. Astrid doesn't exactly look strong with her willowy limbs and graceful-meets-unfocused way of moving through the world. But she holds Marla steady, and opens the bedroom door with her other hand. Marla kicks at Astrid's middle, but Astrid doesn't even stumble. I assume they make it all the way down the hall to Marla's room like that.

"You didn't tell us she was using the bad closet," Eleanor says when we're alone. "What are all these secrets you're keeping? What is going on with you?"

"You don't tell me everything," I say. I want to argue that Marla is totally fine, and Astrid and Eleanor are overreacting, but in the wake of Marla rolling and retching on the ground, we'd both know it was a lie. "You haven't been around. You don't care. You have a whole new family with your secret boyfriend."

Eleanor rolls her eyes. "Wouldn't that be nice?" she says, small, quiet words that sound sad instead of mean. They hurt, but I know she doesn't mean them to hurt me. I think about LilyLee and the way her mom always makes sure she has sunblock and the newest greatest books. How once a summer they go to Canobie Lake Park and ride the rickety roller coasters, the whole three-person family.

If Eleanor's secret boyfriend's family is anything like that, I guess I get it.

"Did you go in the closet too?" Eleanor asks. We are both sitting cross-legged. Our knees are touching. I can hear Astrid and Marla whispering down the hall, and I wonder how it is that Dad hasn't woken up in the midst of all this excitement. I don't answer Eleanor, so she asks again. "Silly. Did you go in? Did you see it? Did you like it? Did you have your special powers in there, too?"

"No," I say. "I didn't like it. I don't like it. But Marla does. Did you see her smile? She was so happy."

"That's not what happy looks like, okay?" Eleanor says. "Maybe you haven't seen it in a while, but that's not it." Eleanor looks sad for me.

Astrid comes back into the room and crawls into her bed. It's not even dinnertime yet.

"Go to Marla's room, Silly," she mumbles. Astrid never calls me Silly, so it hurts. I stand right up; I felt too small sitting like that. "She's sick. And scared. And you wanted to be involved. So go help her." This pinches too. Eleanor opens her mouth. I'm not sure if she means to stand up for me or agree with Astrid, but she changes her mind and purses her lips.

"What if Marla goes back in?" I ask.

"You won't let her," Astrid says. It is final and certain and sleepy.

twenty-five

I don't eat dinner. I don't sleep.

I have to wake Marla up in the morning. I shift around in the bed a lot, after a whole sleepless night here, and clear my throat, and "accidentally" throw my arm into her stomach.

"Oh, sorry," I say when she opens her eyes. There's a brief second of her trying to remember why I'm there, and then she sort of shakes her head like it needs to be cleared out. "You feeling better?" I get out of bed right away. Marla doesn't smell great in the mornings, and the whole room feels small and hot, all close and raw and in need of an open window and a lit candle.

Marla doesn't open her windows or have a collection of sweet-smelling candles in her room.

"Better?" she says like she doesn't understand my question. She scrunches her nose. She must smell and feel how rotten her room is right now too. "Let's get breakfast. You want to go get something? I bet no one's making anything, but we could grab bagels down the street." Marla and I have never gone to the bagel shop together. That's something I used to do with Mom when we were awake before everyone else, back when she was doing well. It was a summer tradition, almost better than the pancakes and bacon on Sundays.

As far as I know, Marla doesn't even like bagels.

"No more bad closet, right? You saw how we almost got stuck?" I'm hanging out near her door, ready to leave as soon as she confirms that she is not crazy. It sounds like Dad is awake. I can hear folky guitar music playing on his extra-special, don't-ever-touch-them speakers.

Marla shrugs.

I'm panicking. It doesn't matter what Dad says. I know Mom's sister got stuck. I know we could all get stuck. I know the closet was writing us a warning.

"I like it in there," Marla says. "Maybe Mom's sister liked it in there too. Maybe Mom would have liked to stay in there. She doesn't seem that happy out here." Marla doesn't look scared. She doesn't look sick anymore either, or sleepy, or angry, or any of the ways I'm used to Marla looking.

"You need to be scared," I say. I'm afraid if I say too much, she will cut me off entirely, but what I want to do is yell at her about safety and insanity and closets and locked doors that never open.

Marla looks at me. It is a hard stare. The kind that doesn't budge, doesn't blink. It is a stare I can feel from my burning face to my tingling toes. I'm not sure what she's looking for, what assessment she's coming up with, but she doesn't say anything else on the subject.

"Bagels," she says instead, just when I think the stare might actually suffocate me. "We definitely need bagels. You like that blueberry cream cheese, right?"

"Right," I say. Marla nods, like we've solved everything, and pushes past me to open the door the rest of the way.

Everyone else is already downstairs. Astrid and Eleanor are opening and closing the fridge like it's a magic trick, where every time you look in again you might find something new. Dad is looking at his paper but flips the pages so quickly I'm not sure he's actually reading it. They are all pajamaed, with fleece jackets unzipped but on, since the door to the porch is wide open and the New Hampshire morning chill is intense today. It's an immediate reminder that it won't be summer forever, that fall is running right behind and will catch up someday soon.

"We're getting bagels!" Marla says. Her voice is too loud for the morning, and more important, too loud to be coming out of Marla. Dad jumps in his chair. The paper makes a startled, rattling sound. Eleanor and Astrid slam the refrigerator door shut again and spin toward us.

"How nice!" Dad says when he recovers his voice. He smiles and looks vaguely proud, like he has somehow brought his daughters closer together in our time of crisis. "You should go get some money from Mom's drawer! Wouldn't that be nice? Like she's buying them for us. She would love that." Mom has a drawer in the kitchen where she throws dollar bills that were shoved in pockets or left on the counter. I hate that one of the only things that might be good about this morning—a hot bagel with blueberry cream cheese—is going to be taken over by Mom, or by Not-Mom, the Mom who exists only in Dad's head.

"I've got it," I say, so that Mom's not the one buying. "Allowance." Dad crinkles his eyes in confusion. He's probably not sure whether to tell me how nice that is, or to insist that we use Mom's money so we don't forget for a minute that she exists.

Eleanor and Astrid zip up their fleeces and remind

Marla and me to get ours, and I guess we're all walking over there together now. Eleanor and Astrid have not smiled.

We should not stop at the mailbox on the way to the bagel store, because I really, really want to actually get a bagel and eat it in peace, to the sounds of Dad's lame folk music and rapid-newspaper-page-turning. I want Marla's mood to stay strangely gleeful for a few hours, and to watch television with my sisters, and maybe even to run down to the lake for a swim and a game of Marco Polo, which Mom tells us is a terrible, dangerous game but which we can't help loving for its loud yelling and splashing and stealthy swimming. Maybe, if we can convince Dad, there will be some hamburgers burned on the public grill at the beach that we haven't used all summer.

I want it to look and feel like summer.

But. We stop at the mailbox.

A package and letter have come for Astrid.

There's a postcard for me that says Mom is proud of me.

There is nothing for Marla.

Astrid reads her letter out loud and overenunciates the part where Mom asks how Marla is doing. Marla sits on the lawn in protest and doesn't look at how huge and ridiculous Astrid smiles. *Look! See! Mom loves you!* her smile says.

"I'm going to my room," Marla says.

"We agreed to go get bagels, so let's do that," Eleanor

says. "I think it would mean a lot to Silly. And we all had a long night taking care of you. So let's do what the family wants now." She crosses her arms. I raise my eyebrows at Astrid, who raises hers back at me.

"I'm okay," I say, because the last thing I want is Marla stomping her way to the bagel place and all the way back and giving me that hard stare she gave me earlier.

"Marla's fine. Everything's fine. We're getting bagels. We're going to eat them in the kitchen together. You can spend the rest of the day in your room, if you want. Now, what else did Mom give you, Astrid?" Eleanor says.

Astrid takes out the little gifts Mom included in her package: a turquoise stone on a small silver chain and a tiny dream catcher with pretty white feathers hanging off it.

"Give them to me," Marla says. There aren't many things I really love about my sister, but I love that she asked outright instead of pretending it is okay to not have received any presents or letters from Mom yet.

"Okay," Astrid says, because Astrid doesn't need anything. Astrid sort of lives in a world where necklaces and dream catchers and sick moms don't really exist anyway.

"You want to talk about it?" Eleanor says. She doesn't sound sympathetic, only matter-of-fact. That's how Eleanor is now.

"We can get the bagels, okay? Happy?" Marla pockets

the little gifts and doesn't say thank you. It's getting too hot for our fleeces. The morning is turning into not-morning, and the sun is summer-strong and we are right in its path.

"You want to talk about Mom not sending you stuff?" Eleanor clarifies, but not very nicely.

Astrid starts walking toward the store. She doesn't have it in her to be part of our fights. Or she really wants bagels.

"I'd be mad, so I don't blame you. No one blames you," Eleanor says. "But you can't throw a tantrum every time you're sad about Mom. We're all dealing with that."

Marla turns around, kicking up some grass. "I'll be inside," she says. The door slams behind her, and Eleanor and I are alone.

Eleanor sits in the grass, taking the place where Marla was.

"Astrid can do it herself," Eleanor says. It surprises me, how quickly the air whooshes out of her, how fast she goes from totally-on-top-of-it adult to defeated little girl. Littler than me. She pulls her knees in to her chest and rests her forehead there. "Wait with me, okay?"

I sit down next to Eleanor. There's a zero percent chance Astrid is going to remember what kind of bagels I like, but there is a one hundred percent chance that she'll come up with something wacky—peanut butter on garlic, cinnamon raisin and salt paired together with cream cheese in between. It's always an adventure with Astrid.

"Does Mom hate Marla?" I say. I always thought Marla was Mom's favorite, but with her bruised wrist and the envelopes without her name on them, I'm starting to think I got it all wrong.

"I think Marla reminds Mom of herself," Eleanor says.

"Is Marla like Mom?" It's the question I can't stop asking in my head, so I might as well ask it out loud now.

Eleanor pulls up a chunk of grass. It's the kind of thing I usually do, not her. "I don't know."

"Have you heard the name Laurel before?" I say. I'm wondering if it's slipped out of Mom's mouth the way so many other things have in bad moments.

Eleanor looks at me almost cross-eyed.

"Sure, we all have. It's on the bench by the lake," she says.

"What bench?" There's the dock and the light playing on the ripples of water and the sticky sand and the not-as-sticky sand, and the minnows that I try not to think about, and the underused grills and the lifeguard stand down a ways, but close enough to watch us.

"The bench," Eleanor says, too irritated to have to explain it to me. "You know. Brown. Wood. Little metal plaque thing that says 'In Memory of Laurel' on it. It's, like, in the grass before the sand. Under the birch tree."

I know the birch tree. I like to rip long pieces of papery white bark from it, even though Astrid says that is bad for the environment.

I guess I can picture a bench, too, but I always sit in the grass or in the sand or on the dock where my legs can dangle into the water. I would never sit on a bench at the beach.

"Mom sits on it a lot," Eleanor says, as though with enough words I'll eventually remember.

"I think Laurel was Mom's sister," I say. I'm tired of all the knots and tangled information I have in my head. I want someone to comb it out for me.

"The dead one?" Eleanor says, like there may be more sisters and more secrets, which I guess wouldn't be that surprising anymore.

"I think she's stuck," I say. "Marla and I think that, maybe. That she's in the closet."

I wouldn't say it if I didn't have my secret star in my jewelry box. I wouldn't say it if I didn't have a little drop of magic just in case Eleanor says we can never go in the closets again.

Eleanor takes a few very deep breaths.

"You know I found Mom in your closet when we first came here," she says at last. I can't tell if she thinks I'm stupid or crazy or right. "She wouldn't come out. She slept in there. It was that night we let you sleep in our room. We didn't want you to see."

"I would have been okay," I say.

"It would make sense, sort of," Eleanor says. "Dad says the best stories are the ones when everything clicks into place, right when it's at its most confusing."

"Laurel," I say.

"Laurel," she says.

One second later, Astrid's in sight.

"I did all berries!" she says, practically skipping toward us with a huge brown bag of bagels. "I combined every kind of fruit cream cheese with every kind of fruit bagel. Blueberry cream cheese on strawberry bagel. Grape jam on raspberry bagel. It's impressive." Astrid's smile makes me smile. It's so big and wide-eyed and out of proportion.

"Sounds like a feast," I say. I want to match Astrid's energy.

"It is!" Astrid says. "We're gonna make today good, okay? We're gonna be okay. All of us." She hands me a bagel. I don't know what it is exactly, but her bright eyes and warm face make me take a huge bite. It's a combination of jam and cream cheese, an explosion of tastes that drips down my chin and onto the grass.

Eleanor giggles. So does Astrid.

I miss Marla even though she's only a few feet away, in the house. I wish she were here for this.

"We'll take it from here," Eleanor whispers, right when I thought we were in it together. She rubs my knee, and I can't believe I'm still stupid Silly to her. It makes me miss Marla even more. "Astrid and I will figure out this whole Mom and Laurel and closets thing."

"Why?" I say. I want her to know I want to be part of it all. That I *am* part of it all.

"You already messed up everything with Marla, honey," Eleanor says. It's the meanest thing she's ever said to me, and she says it so, so nicely.

twenty-six

"There's something I haven't told you," Marla says, choosing a strawberry bagel with raspberry jam.

I've brought a few bagel options up to Marla's room, since she didn't join us for our messy feast in the kitchen. We sit on the floor while she eats. Eleanor left to see her secret boyfriend as soon as she was done eating. Astrid vanished into her room.

"We have to be in this together," Marla says. It makes my heart jump. Marla and me. On a team together. It feels unsteady.

"Eleanor and Astrid don't think of you as an equal. I mean, you know that, right? That's not going to change.

They're twins. You're never going to be one of them." Marla steps closer to me. I try to picture Marla and me having the kind of bond I've always thought I had with Astrid. My face burns. So do my insides. I hear the screen door downstairs slam, and I know Astrid is going on one of her long walks to who-knows-where. And Marla's right. I'm going to be eleven forever and they're going to be fourteen for who knows how long, and I'll never really be an equal.

"You're not going to stop going in the closet, huh?" I say, nicely so Marla knows that I've heard her and agree about Astrid and Eleanor. She puts her hand on my leg, and it's so cold the iciness travels through my pajamas and makes me shiver.

"They can't tell us what to do," she says. I try to nod. I hope my eyes aren't as black as hers. I hope my limbs aren't as cold. I hope I don't have the strange smile that looks more like a frown than anything else. I want to check on my little hidden star, just to remind me of the things in the world that are light and warm and silent and lovely. I need some magic. I need some closet. I need a swim in a silver lake that glitters and a walk through a forest of sunflowers that are taller than pine trees.

"I can trust you now, right? You get it?" Marla's big dark eyes look at me. Even the lashes look darker, longer, thicker, more like spiders and less like feathers.

Star, star, star, I say in my head to stop the pain gathering there, behind my eyes, near my ears, the middle of my neck.

"I don't like it," I say, trying to find the right words. "I don't like Astrid's closet. Or the secrets. Or that Eleanor is out with her secret boyfriend. Or that Astrid isn't up here with us. Or that you didn't eat your bagel downstairs." I can see sun peeking through clouds outside the window. Normally I would think it is beautiful, but right now I can only think of how Astrid's terrible closet might reimagine it. It might turn black or grow so large it takes over the sky, or swallow me whole.

"You know what Eleanor says about you? She says you're too young to be in the closets. She says we should glue yours shut," Marla says. She crosses her arms over her chest. I know Marla well enough to guess that she's bluffing, but it somehow hurts anyway. "It shouldn't surprise you, them saying that. This is how it's always been."

"You miss Mom even though that never changes either," I spit back. It's the kind of thing I would only ever say when I'm not thinking things through, when my filter is off because there was a lot of sugar in the fruity bagels and I haven't slept enough.

"What if we could get Mom back and get Astrid and Eleanor to think of you as not a kid? What if both things were possible?" Marla says. I don't think she believes the second is possible at all, but there's a desperation in her voice, and she cements it after her next deep breath. "I need you," she finishes. "Okay? I need you."

My throat tightens, and I consider crying but think better of it, because Marla won't think I'm strong and capable and mature if I start crying. Then she'll quickly not need me anymore anyway.

"Okay," I say. The tightness in my throat turns to almost suffocation. The last time Marla trusted me, she took me into Astrid's terrible closet. Maybe Marla trusting and needing me isn't the best idea ever. Marla moves closer to me. Lengthens her legs next to mine. She's got on ridiculous Christmas socks that make no sense in July, and she wiggles her toes in them nervously.

"Okay. So. My closet," she says, and stops. It is not a full sentence, so I keep my eyebrows raised and my head tilted in her direction and try to not say *WHAT? WHAT?* over and over again to make her finish.

"The bad closet," I prompt. It's hard to forget about melting walls and too-sharp leaves.

"No. I'm not talking about Astrid's closet now. I'm talking about mine. My closet works too," she says. "I have a special closet too."

I can't help rolling my eyes.

Marla is someone who lies. Or, not quite lies. Marla

believes the things she says even when they are not true. What is the word for that?

I don't know, but when she says she has a magic closet, just like the rest of us, I know it can't be true. Watching someone lie makes me tired, and I'm already so tired from Astrid's closet and missing Mom and hating that I miss Mom, and all the lies and secrets that have been piling up all summer.

"I'm going to take a nap," I say. I will probably not take a nap. I will probably visit my star, then go into my closet. I want to bring a single feather in there and watch it fly as slowly as a lazy river moves. I want to see something ordinary become beautiful, and forget that sometimes ordinary things become evil.

Marla grabs my hand. "It's not like your closet. Or Eleanor's. Or Astrid's. It's a whole other thing," she says. She won't let go of my hand. I try to wiggle my fingers a little, to let her know her tight grip is hurting me, but she only squeezes harder. I wonder if you can pass out from excessive hand holding. Maybe?

"Marla."

"Silly. I mean, Priscilla." She loosens her grip on my hand and takes a deep inhale. "I need you to come inside with me." She lets go of my hand entirely. Clears her throat. Her eyes are going back to their normal color, and her cheeks are returning to a pale pink. There's that ridiculous prettiness again.

"Will I like it?" I say. We are both whispering, our voices going quieter and breathier with every sentence, so that by the time I say this, it is barely audible.

"It's the best thing I've ever seen," Marla says. "And it's going to fix everything."

I shiver. I am icy cold on the inside and boiling hot on the outside, and I know I'm going to go into Marla's closet, but I might need to throw up first.

⁓

Marla and I stand outside her closet door like it will open for us, without our touching it, which of course isn't true. I can hear Marla's breathing, loud and fast, until I realize it is my own breathing I'm hearing.

I open the door myself. I'm scared because Marla scares me lately, but the closet doesn't, because I know Marla's lying. I believe Astrid, and Astrid says this closet's normal. We step inside, and Marla shuts the door behind us. And we wait for a long, long time.

"Your closet is only a closet," I say. I try not to sound mean or judgmental, but the truth is that we are sitting among hanging dresses that are tickling the top of my head and dust bunnies that are surely sticking to my pajama pants, and I don't feel like pretending things are different.

Marla pulls more of Mom's bracelets out of her pockets and puts them on the ground. They sit there, a shimmering pile of promises and words that have lost all their meaning.

"Wait," Marla says. And before she puts the final *T* sound on the word, the closet shifts. It feels like a ride at Disney World, where Dad took us once when Mom was Away and we were so sad we didn't want to celebrate Christmas or eat pancakes or anything. The closet spins and shakes, and if I had to stand up, I would fall right back down from the dizziness. Instead I stay still and close my eyes.

When the spinning stops, the rocking begins.

I don't open my eyes. I want to, but I can't. Marla notices and grabs my hand, pulls me to my feet, and moves my body into a new position. Standing up, bent at the waist, one hand reaching down, down, down. Then I feel it. Water. So warm it could be from a bathtub, but fizzy too. Tiny bubbles shudder and pop against my fingers, spit into the palm of my hand.

Little bubbles pop and fizz in my heart, too.

We are gliding forward, water rushing through my fingers. Marla lets go of my hand, but I keep it trailing along the surface of the water. It's one of those wonderful feelings that fingers get to experience, like reaching into a box of beads at the bead shop in town and letting the tiny plastic circles first swallow and then fall through your fingers.

"Champagne river," Marla says. And I open my eyes at last.

"What is this?"

"It's a memory closet," Marla says. She has happy tears in her eyes, but all I can feel is scared.

There are trees with golden trunks and the river is golden and fizzing. The boat we are somehow in is golden. Marla's eyes are golden.

This isn't a memory, I want to say. *This is a story.* But Marla doesn't seem open for comments right now. Plus, it's hard to have a conversation when you're in a champagne river surrounded by golden trees.

The leaves on the trees are silver and look light enough to drop into our boat at any moment, light enough to be blown away by the breeze.

"It's—," I start. But I want to see the rest of it first. The ballroom. The princes. The worn-through shoes. The floor-sweeping dresses. "It's sort of like the beginning of the fairy tale. It's 'The Twelve Dancing Princesses,'" I say, but Marla already knows.

"You were right," Marla says, and she smiles with her chin out and her eyes sparkling.

"I was right? About us being the princesses?" I touch the top of my head like a crown might have appeared there. There's only frizz.

"Even better. Wait. The castle's coming," she says. Marla picks a flower from a vine hanging overhead. It is the most delicate thing I've ever seen. Gold and crinkled and so fragile she has to hold it only by the very tip of her thumb and forefinger. "It's all like this. Breakable. Crumbling. So be careful." She rubs those two fingers together only the tiniest amount, a small, gentle gesture, but the petals turn instantly to dust, gold fragments floating down to the water.

I fidget uncomfortably in the boat. Try to put as little weight as possible on it. I don't want it to crumble beneath us like that flower.

"What do we do?" I whisper, panic mounting. First Marla brings me into Astrid's terrible closet, and now we are in a vanishing world. A world that will turn to gold flakes if we move at all. I try not to breathe.

Marla laughs. "The boat is fine." She has a little too much delight in her eyes; they are shiny and gold and strange. "And the castle is fine. But everything else, everything beautiful, is crumbling."

"I want to go back," I say. I'm still whispering, just in case my voice carries and its shakiness vibrates and destroys a tree or a bush or a golden bridge.

"We'll go back soon. You have to see first," Marla says. She won't stop smiling. She rubs her knees with her hands, and I hate looking at her hands because then I look at her wrists and then I remember our mother and the bruise that was underneath the bracelets and all the letters Mom chose not to write Marla. And then I have to wonder if there are bruises anywhere else. If maybe I've been missing them all along.

I can't wonder too hard. The palace appears in front of us. Exactly like the fairy tale said it would.

twenty-seven.

I do not turn into a princess the moment the double doors to the palace open. If anything, I turn invisible in the sea of floor-sweeping ball gowns and tuxedos and gold columns and silver silk draping the entire hall. Dozens of people walk by without giving us a second glance. They hold hands and sway to the music and fix their hair as it slips out of complicated knots and braids and buns.

"Where are the princesses?" I'm still mostly concerned with the fairy tale, and my theory that we are living in it somehow. I need to know if that's what is happening to us.

"You have to wait," Marla says.

"How'd you find out your closet works? I thought your

closet was the only one that wasn't magical. When did you try it without us? And why?" Marla is nodding along with the music, but she doesn't answer. More than that, she seems to know what's going to happen before it does. She looks to her right, and a moment later a beautiful woman enters. Marla looks to the left, and on cue, someone starts dancing there.

"It's a memory," Marla says again. "It's a place that holds memories."

"The closets give you what you need," I say, repeating the very first rule I understood, and realizing how desperately Marla wants to know about the past. So badly, apparently, that her closet only shows her things that have already happened. Although I can't imagine why she thinks this is memory and not a fairy tale.

She's counting on her fingers and surveying the ballroom. "Almost time." She nods at the door with a huge grin.

Twelve princesses walk in.

I guess I don't know for sure they are princesses. They certainly don't look like sisters. They are different shapes and sizes and shades. They do have long, wavy hair, all of them, and pretty dresses that they look surprised to be wearing, and thrilled at the prettiness. They walk on tiptoes. They do not have tiaras.

"It's them!" I say. I grab Marla's elbow.

"It's her," she says. She gestures to the last girl in the line of twelve.

Silver shoes. Pale-blue gown. Long chestnut hair. Pale-blue eyes. Sloped nose. Cheekbones even higher than mine.

"That's—" I can't stop looking at her face. Familiar and foreign all at once.

"Mom," Marla finishes my sentence for me.

It is Mom. Before.

Before "unwinding time" and afternoons of sleeping and stringy hair and a puffy face. Before Arizona and Away and moving to the New Hampshire house. Before everything went wrong. Before us.

She is so beautiful.

She looks exactly like Marla, when Marla isn't grumpy.

"I wanted to know when Mom was happiest. And it showed me," Marla says.

"Are there other memories too?" I say. I want to ask if we are in any of her happy memories. But Marla doesn't seem to be thinking about why Mom's happiest times are before we even existed.

"I think so. But I haven't tried. I only want to visit this one."

I want to know everything. I want to visit everything. And I guess I could, but I stay in the memory Marla has chosen for now, knowing I'll be back for more.

Princess Mom wanders farther into the room. The gowns are a forest of taffeta and silk and tulle, and every texture brushes against my arms and tickles. No one looks our way, not even when my arm hits theirs. I feel them, but they can't feel me.

"It gets even better," Marla says when we are in the center of the room, a little lost in all the beauty.

"Is it really her?" I say. I have so many other questions, but I only know how to ask this one.

"I think it has to be. Because . . . look."

I look to where Marla's pointing. Up a staircase that is marble with gold railings and a swooping, curvy shape. It seems to practically reach the ceiling, which is painted with clouds and blue sky and angels and skinny trees with too many leaves.

In the same way the twelve girls paraded into the room, so does a line of boys in puffy shirts and coats with long tails and shoes so shiny they are practically mirrors.

"No," I say, when the last one reaches the bottom of the stairs. I recognize him. "No way."

"And now they dance," Marla says. She is smiling, a whole new Marla, one who is truly happy and squinty-eyed and sweet.

The last boy to make his way down the stairs is my father. He doesn't look as different as my mother does. His hair is a little blonder and more filled in on top. He doesn't have a shadow of stubble on his chin or little lines around his eyes. But otherwise, he's Dad.

My mother and my father are dancing in a room of gold and crystal and marble and magic. Dad has one arm around Mom's waist, and the other arm is held high in the air with her hand in his. They are straight-backed and shiny-haired. They are perfect dancers. Neither of them so much as looks at their feet. They are too busy staring at each other to look anywhere else. They are falling in love in front of our eyes.

They are the people Dad reads about in books. They are their own fairy tale.

"This is why Mom is going to be fine," Marla says. I was going to say the opposite. This is why Mom doesn't like the life she's living now.

"Mmm," I hum in response, so that I don't lie but I also don't let her down too hard. "How'd Dad get in here?" I say. My mind is flooded with information and confusion, and I have to swim through it a bit. "I mean, Mom makes sense—it was her closet when she was little. But why is Dad in here?"

"It's a fairy tale. Don't ask so many questions," Marla says. "That's what Dad would say, right?"

She's wrong, of course. Dad would say the opposite. It's a fairy tale, so think about every little bit of it really, really hard. Marla doesn't get him at all.

But I wish I could feel how Marla does right now: like the details and reasons don't matter because it's all so pretty and romantic and nice. But with my drowning mind and my pounding heart and my open eyes I think of all the times Dad has strangely avoided telling us where he's from. I think of the Mets hat that isn't because he loves New York and the fact that we don't have aunts or uncles or grandparents. That all we have from his family is that one beautiful magical-looking mirror.

I think of all the fairy tales Dad loves and the way that they are sometimes more important to him than anything else, than real life. That he can understand every nuance of "Sleeping Beauty" or the myth of Echo and Narcissus, but not his own daughters, not my mother, not the way real life is falling to pieces.

"Dad isn't from the real world," I say.

I want to rush at them, and I suppose I could, but they wouldn't see me. We are spectators here. In the other closets we are everything, but here we are nothing. We are meant to watch, but not meant to participate.

Another one of the twelve princesses sweeps past me. Her full skirts hit my legs with such force I trip and fall. It would be embarrassing if anyone could see. But they can't. I scurry back into a standing position and hold Marla's hand as our parents dance circles around everyone else.

It makes perfect sense and no sense at all. Dad's from a fairy tale. Of course he is. He's got that perfect jaw and nice laugh and never-ending vat of hope and a belief in happily-ever-after in his heart and an endless knowledge of princesses and stories we tell and dragons and magic.

I miss my father.

And also, I miss my mother. Not the way I miss LilyLee when I haven't gotten a letter in a while. Not the way I have missed my home since we moved away. I miss my mother in a place further down than that. I miss a version of her that I've seen so rarely over the years that I can't even remember her. I miss her Before, teasing my father about his goatee and playing freeze tag in the backyard with us, and sewing outfits for my stuffed animals with scrap fabric.

I miss the mother who is dancing with my father in front of me, so close I could touch her, I could hide under the draping of her dress. I miss the mother who was so brave and sure that she would steal a prince from a magical palace and bring him to the real world. I miss the mother who cared so much about love and happiness and wonder, even though I think I never knew her. I miss this look on her face that I've maybe never seen before: sweet and excited and something else. Enchanted. Words I would never use to describe the mother I have now.

"This is just a fairy tale, though," I say. I don't like Marla thinking we can save Mom, or that we can get this version of our mother to move from her closet to our house. "This isn't who she is anymore."

"You're not seeing the most important part," Marla says. She points to another princess, a shy, small one not dancing with boys.

One in a blue dress who looks a little like Mom and a little like Marla and a lot like me.

"Laurel!" Mom says, shouting from Dad's arms. "I'm dancing with you next!" The girl who looks like me smiles. I wonder if this is what fainting feels like. Dizzy and weak and breathless.

"I know about your star," Marla says before I can say anything. I hug myself at the mention of my star. No one is supposed to know about it. I panic, wanting it here right now. I want to get out of the conversation and maybe even the closet, but Marla's on a mission. "If you can bring that star out of the closet, why not Laurel?"

"I don't know what—," I start, but the look in her eyes stops me. It would be stupid to finish my sentence. She's seen it. She knows.

"Silly," she says. That's it. Just my name. Or my not-name.

"The star is something else. It's special." The lights in the ballroom dim a little. Candelabras and chandeliers and lanterns hanging from every doorway all darken enough so that the room quiets down. The music lowers too. There is a hush, but the dancing doesn't stop.

"She's special," Marla says. "Mom's been looking for her this whole time. We have to bring her out."

"She's not like the star. She's a person. A memory."

"Why don't you care about Mom?" Marla says.

Young Dad spins Young Mom. Again and again, so much that I think she must be getting dizzy. Mom doesn't lose her step, not once. She finishes in his arms, pressed against him for a moment, and when they resume their dancing stance, they're both sort of blushing. I have to look away. It feels like something private, something I'm not meant to see.

"I'll think about it," I say, picturing Mom and Dad dancing in our living room to some old-time song on the radio. It would be nice. Embarrassing but nice.

"Couldn't you watch this all day?" Marla says. "We could get her back. That's our mom."

Marla's content to watch only this moment, but I need to know so much more before I'll know how I feel about it. There's another tug of longing for that mother, especially when she breaks apart from Dad to go back to her sister. She combs Laurel's hair with her fingers and whispers secrets in her ear.

We can hear them talking. Mom's voice is higher and sweeter. Marla nudges me to listen more carefully, because she's heard it all before and wants me to feel and think the same way she does.

"Let's stay here forever," Mom says to Laurel.

"Let's bring him out with us," Laurel says. "Would that help you?"

"You know I can't," Mom says. "We tried with the silver leaves and those amazing pastries."

Laurel grins, and I feel like I'm looking at myself in a mirror. She can do it. She can bring him out if she wants to. She looks the way I felt when I took the star out. She looks the way I feel about that secret, and I know that she has the same secret.

Marla knows it too.

"You can bring people out," Marla whispers. "They did it. You can do it for Mom."

The scene fades, the world reorganizing around us, and a moment later we are at the same ball but with different dresses, different music, bigger flower arrangements, more chandeliers.

"What did you do?" Marla says. She knocks the side of her body against the side of mine, a Marla-shove that makes me stumble. I don't respond to her hitting me, because when she's like this it's pointless to argue with her. Like when

Mom has had a lot to drink or is recovering from having had a lot to drink or really anytime at this point.

"I wanted a different memory," I say. "I was curious, and I guess the closet was listening to what I wanted—"

Marla goes for the door. She doesn't want to see more than the prettiest moment. But I catch a glimpse of what I was wondering about, before she's able to get through the crowds to the place we entered. There's Laurel and Dad, holding hands, walking to the closet door together. She took him out for her sister. She tried to save Mom too.

Then the door's open and Marla is slapping at my arms.

"We have to save her, we have to save her," she says over and over until snot is dripping from her nose and she runs out of breath.

She doesn't stop swatting at me. And I let her. It's what she needs.

twenty-eight

I hold my star in my hand before I go to bed and the next morning before I go downstairs. It is the perfect kind of warm: not skin-burning heat, but hot enough to get a little beneath my surface. I am holding something strong and powerful.

I squeeze it and it pulses back at me.

Something in my head lightens, releases, lets go. And the world brightens, tightens, leaps to life.

I wore glasses for a few weeks last year. Then I broke them, and I was scared Mom would get mad if I told her. No one remembered I'd ever needed glasses, so I didn't get in trouble, but I didn't get new ones, either. But. For those few weeks that I wore them, even though I looked like a total loser, I loved the world a little more. The colors looked brighter. The shapes were sharp and perfect: circles were perfect circles. Right angles were deliberate and satisfyingly straight. I felt like I understood things about the world, that with those glasses on I was seeing so much more and appreciating more and becoming a new person.

Anyway, that's a fraction of how I feel with the star in my hand. The harder I squeeze, the clearer and newer and more beautiful everything is. In a few breaths, I feel like I can manage the day, whatever happens. I can manage the memories from Marla's closet yesterday and Astrid's closet before and missing Mom and having to eat Pop-Tarts and cereal and pizza for dinner every night.

I maybe don't even need to go into my closet. I have the UnWorry now. In my hand.

———◦———

"Who wants to talk to Mom?" Dad says when I'm in the TV room eating my least favorite flavor of Pop-Tart. We are all out of delicious cinnamon. I'm stuck with fake strawberry, which is good, but I'd rather have pancakes.

I rush to his side and he jumps; he'd been preparing himself for the usual quiet and stillness that follows that question. "Silly?" he says. It's the first time I've seen him since watching him yesterday as a young man wooing my mother, and it's strange, to have that between us now. To know that he once lived in a magical closet and now he lives out here with us. And I guess we make him happy, even though there are no golden trees or turrets or taffeta. And that's nice, that he loves his life with us so much that he's forgotten about his life Before.

Marla, curled up on a chair across the room, gives me a *shut up* look, but I ignore it. We didn't talk after we left her closet yesterday, after she finally stopped hitting me. Instead we stayed in our separate rooms and took separate bike rides around the neighborhood and didn't speak when Astrid ordered pizza for us to eat so that Dad could go to some dinner meeting at the university.

"You're ready to talk on the phone with her?" Dad says, catching some kind of hesitation in the way I'm slow to reach for the phone, and, probably, the way I'm staring down Marla.

"Yep," I say, and take the phone from his hand. The cell service is bad, and if I move around too much the call will drop, so I'll be stuck talking to her in the middle of the room. He rubs his head in confusion, like that will somehow dislodge the thoughts and force my actions to make sense. "Can I do it alone, though?" Dad nods with knitted eyebrows and a frown that's not sad but is thoroughly flabbergasted.

"Uh-huh, of course," he says, and his head keeps on nodding. I nod at Marla, too, asking her with my chin and my eyes to leave the room. Eleanor and Astrid left the instant Dad asked who wanted to talk to Mom, thinking, I guess, that if they left the room they wouldn't have to officially say no. "Remember. She's not one hundred percent herself yet, okay? She might sound a little spacey, but don't worry about that." I remember from other times Mom's been Away that it takes a little while for her to sound like herself again. They put her on some medicine that helps her but also makes her sound a little like she's half dreaming. It's maybe the reason we don't like talking to her on the phone very much when she's Away.

Part of the reason.

Dad closes the swinging door connecting the TV room to the kitchen, Marla scampers upstairs, probably to listen in from the upstairs hallway, which hangs over the TV room, but for now I am alone with the phone and the number Dad already tapped in. I press Talk, and the receptionist puts me through to some hallway phone that I guess the people living there are allowed to use.

Mom answers so fast that I know she's been waiting there for a while.

"You're there," I say.

"I'm here," Mom says.

I have to inhale and exhale before speaking again.

"I saw you last night," I say, because I am terrible at openings.

"It's so good to hear your voice," Mom says at the same time, missing my sentence that makes no sense.

"You and Dad. The fairy tale. The princesses. The closet." This is not going well. "Laurel."

"Silly . . . ," Mom says. She sounds tired more than anything, even though Dad says part of what she is in Arizona for is "rest." I'm waiting for her to sound fully awake. I'm waiting for her to be the way she looked in Marla's closet last night.

"Mom."

"I want you to tell me about the lake," she says. "And LilyLee. And what you have been drawing and writing and watching and listening to. I want to know who is winning the most often at Monopoly and which of your sisters you are angry at today and whether or not you've made any new friends, and . . ." Mom's getting kind of breathless at this point, and she's run out of things to say or maybe is waiting for me to break in and start gossiping away, but that's not why I took the phone from Dad.

"We went into Marla's closet. And saw things. We've *been* seeing things. And I need to know if Laurel is really dead or if she's stuck. And how she got stuck. And I understand why you're so sad and we want to help you, but I'm not sure how. But Marla thinks she knows. Would you want Laurel back, if we could bring her? Is that what we're supposed to do?" I haven't said this much to Mom in months.

"Marla's closet . . . ," she says, part dreamy, part confused. "You know, that was my closet when I was little." I feel the cusp of her believing or maybe remembering, but then it pulls away. It's a wave in an ocean: lapping my feet one moment, drifting away, lost forever the next. "Is that a new game you're playing?" There's a flutter of sound in the background, and the connection gets fuzzy.

"No! The closet!" I yell, bringing my mouth close to the phone. "We see things in there! Things I don't understand!"

"You're not in my closet, are you? Not the closet in the sewing room?" Mom sounds panicked. "That one's locked, Silly. You can't go in there, okay? No going in the sewing room. I've always told you that." Her voice shakes. I can hear other patients in the background asking her to get off the phone. They only have a few minutes of phone time a day, since they share the one hallway phone after their cell phones are taken away. I guess those are the types of things I'm usually trying to forget.

"You're not listening!" I say. Marla has appeared by my side. I hadn't noticed her coming down the stairs. Eleanor and Astrid are there too. All of them, suddenly, pulling at my elbow, at my hand, at my fingers, trying to get the phone away from me.

"What are you *doing*?" Eleanor whispers, pinching the skin of my arm so hard I almost *do* drop the phone.

"Mom. I know you know what I'm talking about. 'The Twelve Dancing Princesses.' The magical closets. The bad closet. Your sister. What do we do?" I say, trying to hold on to the phone while my sisters wrestle me to the ground.

Marla manages to get the phone out of my hands, and she runs to stand on the coffee table while she distracts Mom with talk of the raccoons that have been digging into our garage late at night and the color she wants to paint her room when Mom gets back. It must work, or Mom's phone time runs out, or Marla has wandered into a spot without cell service, because soon Marla's off the table, and I'm still on the ground, and everyone's yelling at me.

"What were you thinking, telling her that?" Marla says.

"She's confused. You can't tell her that stuff *now*. She's, like, on medicine. The kind you were on when you broke your ankle. The loopy, weird kind," Eleanor says, shaking her head.

"You probably freaked her out!" Astrid says. "You freaked us out!"

"You can't make decisions without us. We're doing this together. You can't . . . we brought you in because we trusted you. . . ." Eleanor gets up and starts pacing the room. I'm almost surprised Dad hasn't come back in from the porch, but that's what he's like lately. He wouldn't notice if we burned the house down, probably. He's not going to notice some loud voices and bumping bodies.

Eleanor lets out an end-of-the-world, end-of-her-patience sigh. It is long and loud and smells like orange juice and toothpaste.

"I think we should stay away from the closets altogether," she says at last.

"Stay away!?" I can't control the screech in my voice. The last thing we need to do is stay away. We need to go in more, to learn more, to figure it all out.

"Of course you want to stay away," Marla says.

Eleanor crosses her arms over her chest and rolls her eyes. "Everyone calm down. We can go to the lake when we're sad. Or watch movies. Or make sundaes. We don't need the closets."

"Now that you have your secret boyfriend you don't need them," I say. I'm so sick of Eleanor and the way she wants to control everything but also not be part of anything. I can't stand the new way she dresses. The happy way she practically skips out of the house to see him. Her cell phone strapped to her hand at all times like a security blanket. "You're in love," I say. "You don't need tulips growing from the sky. You have a *boyfriend*. You don't need closets. Or us."

Eleanor blushes. Hard.

I know the look. It's the look you get when someone says something true, but you don't want it to be true. Something true that you haven't admitted is true. Eleanor's face twists through embarrassment and discomfort into anger and defensiveness.

"That's insane," she says. "That's the stupidest thing I've ever heard. Why would you even say something like that? It's *mean*."

"Silly's right," Marla says, looking too proud of herself.

"I . . . think Priscilla's right too," Astrid says in her smallest voice. A mosquito buzzes against the window screen, and the birds sing outside and wind blows the leaves in the trees. Eleanor looks to Astrid like she's never seen certain things about her before, and maybe she hasn't.

Eleanor straightens her shorts so they sit correctly on her waist. She smooths her hair. She runs her hands down the sides of her shirt. And she leaves.

twenty-nine

Eleanor does not come back. She calls in the early evening and asks Dad if she can stay over at her friend Jodi's house, and he says yes. LilyLee's mom would have made sure to get on the phone with Jodi's parents to check that everything was okay with them. LilyLee's dad would have asked a bunch of questions and brought over cookies for her to share with her friend and told her what time he would pick her up in the morning.

Marla passes me a note like we're in class and not at home. It says, *We should tell Dad about the secret boyfriend. We should tell MOM.*

I almost say yes, because when I'm angry I want to

do something big. But instead I shake my head. Not hard enough probably, because Marla looks like she still might do it.

Dad tells us to order whatever we want. We've had so much pizza and Chinese food that we decide to try Indian, even though none of us have ever had it and Dad will probably hate it. He doesn't like much of anything when it comes to food. When the food arrives, it smells delicious and tastes even better. Dad has a few bites of chicken and asks about our day. I want to ask him, too, about what I saw in the closet, but Marla sits on one side of me and clamps her hand down on my thigh whenever I open my mouth to say anything at all.

"Where's Eleanor?" Marla says, her voice all fake-innocent and her eyelashes fluttering like a cartoon character.

"With a friend," Dad says.

"Oh, that boy?" Marla says. Astrid kicks her. Not subtly. Not under the table. Full-on kicks her, in the shins, hard enough that Marla cries out and hugs her leg to her chest.

"A boy?" Dad says. He sounds like a person waking up from a very intense dream who doesn't quite know what's going on. "Eleanor is with a girlfriend. She doesn't know any boys here. None of you do. No boys. Your mom says."

"She's not with a boy!" Astrid says. Her voice is

desperate, the way it sounded when she fought with Mom about Henry. I remember sitting on the stairs in the Massachusetts house, watching Mom and Astrid battle it out.

"You have to take care of your sisters!" Mom said, yelling so loud I swear the house shook. "You can't run around with boys! You have to be a good sister. You think you're so great you can just run off and leave your family to do whatever you want? That's not how it works." Then Mom started crying, which she always did during fights. It made them so unfair. "You hate us. You don't care about us. You're irresponsible." This was the worst, when Mom started listing things that seemed irrelevant and strange, a pile of feelings she insisted we felt, interpretations of things we said that she was positive were exactly right. Arguing made it worse.

But Astrid stood up for herself.

"My sisters don't need me watching their every move. They're not stupid. They're not going to wander into the middle of a street or off a cliff! I'm a good sister. I'd never let them get hurt. But what I'm doing isn't hurting anyone. I love Henry!"

Then the part I never think about happened.

Eleanor was in her room, listening from there. Marla was listening from the basement. But I saw it from the stairs.

Mom pushed Astrid. One hand on each shoulder. One

hard slam. I looked away before Astrid hit the wall. I looked away before I could see how bad it hurt.

And because I'm a truly terrible sister, I didn't say anything about it to anyone.

From the way Dad's shaking, and the tone of his voice when he tells us not to joke about boys around Mom, I think he remembers it too. I think he saw what I saw, a year ago.

I hate my memories. I hate the person I am, the one who turns away and hides. The one who could save everyone but doesn't.

I think Marla hates that part of me too. They probably all do.

I have not had a chance to look at my star since early morning, and the effects are wearing off. I have a headache, and suddenly I'm hating eating with plastic forks and knives. I'm hating these new spices and the yellow of the curry and the red of the rice. I'm hating the sound of the television—Mom would never have let us watch this much—and the sick feeling in my stomach when I think too hard about the drowsiness of her voice on the phone today. When I think too hard about anything at all, to be honest.

◦────ℓ◦

Much later, when I should be asleep, I stay up reading different versions of "The Twelve Dancing Princesses" and looking for clues about my father. Some illustrations look a little like him, but none of them describe what he's like or what to do if you find out your father's from a fairy tale.

After midnight I hear Marla's door squeak, the floor creak, and her footsteps traveling past the stairs, past my room, down the hallway. Toward the bad closet. I can practically feel the chill and the darkness and the pinch of whatever terrible creature might be buzzing around in there.

I listen to the way she sounds on her tiptoes, an almost not-sound that is really socks against carpet. I hear the almost not-click of the twins' door opening. She is nearly perfect at doing it soundlessly, but not quite. I grip my sheets. My chest is tight and my fists are tighter, and I should definitely stop her before she goes in there. But instead I scrunch my toes so that my feet basically become fists too. I watch the curtains make waving shadows on the ceiling. I think about my star in the jewelry box across the room and picture it glowing at me, keeping me calm.

I hope that Astrid will wake up, but I know she's a heavy sleeper and Marla is excellent at being stealthy and silent.

I do not follow Marla into the bedroom. I don't save her from the closet.

I try to talk my body into leaving the bed, but I can't.

It's stuck. A thousand pounds or so of fear are keeping me down.

It's not like I didn't know I was afraid of Astrid's closet. I mean, obviously I am. Any sane person would be scared of that closet. But I didn't realize I had the kind of paralyzing, gray-colored, dizzying fear that I used to only have for snakes and the shows Mom sometimes watches on TV about murderers who look like elementary school teachers.

I stay awake for an hour at least, waiting to hear Marla's featherlight feet tiptoe back to her room.

I'm a terrible, terrible sister, for not going in there to stop her. Or join her. Or do something, ever, to help someone. Like, really. I'm the worst.

thirty

The next morning, Dad makes pancakes, which is alarming since it's Thursday and not Sunday at all.

"We're going to visit your mother!" he announces. He puts a Mickey Mouse pancake on my plate, and what I think is supposed to be a dog pancake on Astrid's plate. He manages a pretty good heart pancake for Eleanor, who got back early from "Jodi's." Dad seems unconcerned with everything but the shapes of the pancakes and Mom. He is always, always very concerned with Mom.

I wonder what would happen if I visited the memory version of him in Marla's closet and told him all my worries. Would he be more helpful? Would he get it? Would he be a different kind of Dad, like LilyLee's, who checks on her grades and asks a million questions when we go to the mall, and pulled me aside once when LilyLee was sad about another friend to ask if I could tell him what was going on because he was so worried.

"No, thank you," I say. I take a bite of the Mickey Mouse pancake's ear.

"That was an announcement, not a question, Silly," Dad says. He keeps a smile on his face, but I am pretty sure there's a frown hidden underneath.

"I can stay here with the girls," Eleanor says, like she is forty and not Astrid's twin.

"I'm not leaving you alone in the house," Dad says. He laughs, to show how zany he thinks we're being and that we are obviously not serious. "You all going nutty? Don't you miss your mom?" Astrid shakes her head, but that's only because she has forgotten to listen to the whole rest of the conversation. "You can go to the lake today while I get all the details settled," he says. "We're going to leave in a few days. None of you have ever seen that part of the country. It will be wonderful."

I think about the Arizona postcards. The ridiculous amount of brown and tan and brownish tan. The prickly cactuses that seem to replace trees there.

"I would miss trees," I say. "We need trees. To breathe and stuff. And also, stability." *Stability* is a word the school counselor used when we all talked with her last year when Mom wasn't doing well. She kept saying it over and over to Dad, until he started repeating it too. Their whole conversation was just a repetition of that one word. Pretty weird.

"Oh, you'll like the trees there!" Dad says, missing the point entirely. "Very different! Sparse. Unique." He nods. At least he agrees with himself. The rest of us clearly do not agree with anything he's saying.

"We're not going," I say. It is not usually up to me to speak for all of us. That's Eleanor's job. But I'm older now. I'll be twelve in two months and three days.

I want to explain why it's impossible to leave: not only am I not ready to see Mom with her bracelets piled on one wrist and some new sunny attitude or something, but we also have the closets to worry about. And the girl who's stuck inside. And the way they save me from how impossible every day seems otherwise.

If I really want to see Arizona, I'll have Astrid make a diorama of it for Eleanor's closet.

"I have postcards," I say. "I know what it looks like. And how Mom is. We talked. So, I think I'm good. And I like the postcards." I emphasize the words *postcards* like it is going to have some very deep impact on Dad. He laughs, but stops when I don't laugh along.

"We're a family, Silly," he says carefully. He gives me another pancake. He is definitely convinced pancakes are the key. "Now, where's Marla? I know she'll be excited." I look around and take count. It's not like I have seventy-five sisters or anything. I'm not even one of twelve. But sometimes I have to list us out to realize who is missing. *Silly, Eleanor, Astrid*, I say in my head, making sure to count myself, because I am always the first person I forget.

I look up at Astrid and Eleanor, to see if they have been doing the same calculation I've been doing, but they're quicker and faster and older, so they've already cleared their plates and run up the stairs, and Dad is looking like he wants to scold them, but can't because they put their dishes in the sink like they're supposed to.

"We better not have this very important conversation without Marla," I say in the least-desperate voice I can muster, which is still very, very desperate. I run up the stairs and straight into Astrid and Eleanor's room, because that is the one and only place everyone would be.

Eleanor is banging on the closet door. She's jiggling the doorknob, yanking and pushing and trying to force the doorknob to turn. I am remembering the terrible paralyzed feeling from last night, and wondering why, why, why I didn't jump out of bed and drag Marla kicking and screaming from Astrid's bad closet into my good one.

"She. Last night. I didn't. When you were. But she must have come out," I say, and then realize I have mostly said words and not sentences. "She went in last night. I heard her. I assumed she came out after I fell asleep! I should have stopped her, but she was so mad at me and I didn't want her to yell and—"

"You heard her go in again?" Eleanor says. She repeats herself, but screeching this time.

"Silly!" Astrid says. Silly. Not Priscilla. If I don't get it together soon, if I don't turn into a much better sister and person, like, ASAP, there will be no one left in the world who calls me by a real name.

Astrid's the one who was asleep in the room when Marla went in. But I'm the one who will get all the blame. Astrid is allowed to be sleepy and spacey, but I'm not allowed to do anything wrong ever.

"What about getting stuck?" Eleanor says. Then they're both banging on the door, and their voices are higher and scarier and scratchier, and I am banging too, and the closet is not opening. Dad knocks on the bedroom door. Thank goodness we closed it behind us.

"Girls? It's a little loud. Are you being mean to Marla?" he says.

"We'll be quieter!" Eleanor calls out. "We're playing!"

"Well. Okay. But we need to finish our conversation," Dad says. He still doesn't open the door. It's some kind of miracle, the way he trusts us.

"Totally! Can't wait!" Astrid says. She sounds more like Eleanor than herself, but desperate times call for desperate measures, I guess. We stay quiet, listening to Dad make his way back downstairs. We start banging again when we're sure he's gone.

"I'll come out when I'm done," Marla says from inside the closet. "I'm almost done, I'm almost done!" Her voice is wet. Teary. Catching on itself and tripping itself up. "Let me be! Leave me here! Everything's fine." It's a relief to hear her voice. All three of us stop for a moment, inhale and exhale deeply.

"Come out now!" Eleanor says. She cups both her hands around her mouth and leans in close to the crack between the door and the wall, like that extra bit of sound that will poke through could make all the difference in saving Marla.

"I like it in here," Marla says, her voice a little farther away, no longer right at the door. I can't stop rubbing my own forehead. *I did this. I did this*, I say inside my head over and over until the words sort of stop being words.

"Marla? Come out? Please?" For a moment I think me asking her will make all the difference. She said we were a team, after all. She said she trusted me. I lean in closer to the closet door and listen for a sound of approval, listen for the turn of the doorknob, but there's only silence.

"I'm not coming out. But I can let you in, if I want you in," Marla says. It's getting harder to hear her. "Someone who won't break the magic. Silly. I want Silly."

"Silly will go in, then," Astrid says. I don't look up from the doorknob, where I've been focusing all my energy, hoping it's going to turn at last and let Marla out. "Silly. Go in and get her," Astrid says, louder now.

Eleanor clears her throat and shares a look with Astrid.

"It can only be you, Silly, she's right. You have to go in," Eleanor says. Coming from Eleanor it's a command, it's the thing I have to do. "If Marla feels like she needs you, I think the closet will maybe let you in. And the closet might listen to you and your needs too. You have your special powers, right?"

"If Marla wants you in there, you'll be able to get in," Astrid says, nodding too much.

"I hate it in there," I say. Eleanor nods and Astrid pulls me into a hug, but neither of them tells me that I don't have to go. "I'm not like Marla. I don't like that closet," I say into Astrid's shoulder.

"Oh! I have something!" Astrid says, releasing me from her arms too suddenly, so that I trip a little from having to stand up alone. Astrid goes to her bed, with its patchwork quilt and too many pillows, and reaches underneath, pulling out a brand-new diorama.

It is in a white box, the kind that is shiny and probably from the most expensive store in Boston. The kind of box you couldn't even find in New Hampshire, because in New Hampshire things don't come that fancy. Inside Astrid has created a tiny world that is gentle and clean and light pink and blindingly white.

"You can do something. With your closet powers. You have to," Eleanor says. She doesn't sound as sure as she usually sounds.

"Wow," I say, and reach my fingers inside to touch the cotton balls that Astrid must have pulled apart to create the snowy veil on the bottom. She's sprinkled glitter on top, so that the snow is impossibly pretty and magical, and not the cruel, cold kind that comes late in February or even in March and gives a mean, wet chill.

"I've been saving it," Astrid says. Aside from the glittering cotton snow, there're also tiny flowers made out of tissue paper, all baby pink and not quite bloomed. There's pink lace on the sides of the box, and a familiar pale fabric cut up in strips and coiled into pretty spiral shapes in all four corners. It's glued in, so I can't take it out to look more closely, but I use my pinkie to trace the soft fabric, and bring the box closer to my face for a better look.

"That's your baby blanket," I say, my head still partially inside the box.

"Good memory," Astrid says. It's not memory, though. Astrid has had her baby blanket on her bed since she was actually a baby. It's silky and soft and worn and familiar. "I wanted it to be a box of everything safe and pretty. I don't know if my closet does anything with dioramas, but probably with you in there, you can make something happen. I figure those things won't go bad in the closet. They're too gentle and good. And you too, Priscilla. You can't go bad either." She says this last bit so quickly, so quietly, I think I must have misheard her. I know that soft white snow and tiny pink barely budded flowers and the softest most-loved bit of blanket have a kind of purity that Astrid has to believe in. But I am not something soft and pretty and familiar. I have pin-straight hair and awkward elbows and ears that are a little too big for my face and cheeks that are a little too pink to be cute the way they were when I was a baby.

I want to say all this, but Astrid and Eleanor are both

looking at me with identical expressions. I think it might be hope.

Hope that I will fix everything.

If not everything, then at least this. I will fix Marla or the closet or both.

thirty-one

Before the closets, I was never the special sister. Eleanor is special because she is smart and beautiful and knows how to do everything without ever having to officially learn how to do it. Astrid is special because she is creative and strange and lives on her own pretty Astrid planet. Marla is special because she demands attention and is like the very important sick child, even though she isn't actually sick. She's the one we all feel bad for.

I'm the one they protect but don't think of as a whole person. I'm the one who sees things and does nothing to help. I'm the one who is Silly.

Until now.

"You can do this," Astrid says. "We've seen what you can do, remember?" I shiver when Astrid says this, because I know it means I won't be able to just pull Marla out by the wrist or elbow. I think Marla has to want to come out, and I'm not sure she does.

But a small part of me thinks maybe Astrid's right. That if anyone can help, it's me. I remember Astrid not being able to get onto the petals of the tulips and Marla not able to get on the boat in the fairy tale in my closet, and the way the memory closet shifted when I wanted it to, even though Marla didn't want it to. And maybe I am something special. Maybe I can do something, finally, to help.

"I'm coming in, Marla," I say. Astrid and Eleanor visibly relax.

"Silly? That's you?" Marla's voice is closer again. She must be near the door, but still under a canopy of black, wilting, aggressive trees. My eyes sting with the beginnings of tears. I want to be brave enough to do this.

"Just me," I say, and turn the doorknob. The knob spins, but the door doesn't open.

I pull again, harder. Twist harder. Twist and pull at the same time. Twist first, pull second. Pull first, twist second. I don't know if my magic is supposed to open it, or Marla's want for me to be there, but nothing has changed.

The door doesn't budge. I use both my hands and reach

down in my stomach for the world's biggest grunt, and pull so hard I worry my shoulders will break away from my arms. At first, I'm almost pleased. If the door doesn't open, I don't have to go inside. My shoulders relax. My eyes stop watering. My mouth lets me swallow again.

It takes only a few seconds, though, before I realize not being able to get inside is the worst thing, not the best. If the door still won't open, it means Marla doesn't really want me in there with her. She wants to be alone. She wants to be trapped.

"Why aren't you opening the door?" Astrid says. "Marla wants you inside. You should be able to get inside. Marla said—"

"Marla doesn't know that much either!" I say. The twins have forgotten that none of us know that much. That we're all still figuring it out. They want to believe one of us knows something Special and Important. But we don't.

"I'm trying," I say. I pull again, this time with my knees bent, and I jiggle the knob back and forth. I sort of know it won't work, but I can't stop doing it.

"That's not working," Eleanor says, like she has figured everything out.

"Hello?" Marla says in a small voice. The knob is alternately hot and cold, but never turning.

"Fine, you try," I say. I don't know why I am suddenly

angry with Eleanor and Astrid, but it's easier than being angry at the door.

Eleanor and Astrid look at each other again. I'm getting tired of knowing that they have a plan that I'm not in on.

"What?" I say, loud and annoyed this time.

"Are you coming in?" Marla says. She sounds like she is moments away from sleep.

"Maybe you can let me in?" I say. I don't want to alarm her. But I'm pretty sure that only she can choose to let me in. And I'm pretty sure she's choosing to not let me in. Somehow she doesn't know it herself.

Stuck, stuck, stuck, the scared voice in my head says. That voice sounds a whole lot like Mom.

"Mmmmm," Marla says. The door shudders a little but doesn't open.

"Don't fall asleep! Are you falling asleep?" I shout through the door.

"It won't open . . . ," Marla says in her sleepiest voice. Singsongy. "You do it."

"We're, um, trying," I say. "It's like before, Marla. When I was in there with you. You said that happens sometimes, right? Sometimes it won't open, but then it does, so let's just wait a second. But don't fall asleep. You sound like you're falling asleep." I pull the door again, lightly, like that might make all the difference.

"Before?" Astrid says.

"You got stuck before?" Eleanor says. "When you went in there, you couldn't get out?"

"For a second. A minute. Then it let us out," I say.

"You didn't tell us that part," Eleanor says. "The closet shouldn't be able to keep you in there. Not ever."

I nod. And shrug. And blush. And trip myself up over an explanation for why I didn't mention it.

"But it was fine," I say. "This happens. And it's fine. It will open in a minute. Or like ten, I bet. Ten minutes. Bam." I want Eleanor and Astrid to nod enthusiastically, believing me.

They don't. But we wait ten minutes anyway. We try to keep Marla awake by singing snippets of songs we know she likes, and forcing her to sing along on the other side of the door. But partway through, her voice gets even quieter and slower and stranger.

Marla doesn't sound so much like she needs me in there anymore. She doesn't sound like she wants me. She doesn't even sound like Marla.

It reminds me of the way Mom gets sometimes. The terrible transition from normal to slower-than-normal to not-normal-at-all.

"It's so dark and cloudy in here," she says, after a rousing rendition of "Rudolph the Red-nosed Reindeer," which is not at all season-appropriate, but at least we know the words. "It smells like sleep. And like burning wood. And it's telling me to rest. So I'm gonna do that. You guys go do your thing. I can take a nice long nap in here." I try the door again. I don't like the way her voice has slowed down so much that it's all distorted and wrong-sounding. I don't like that she isn't trying to get out, that she isn't concerned.

"If she doesn't want to get out, the closet won't let her out," Eleanor says. She's right. It's how the closets work. They give you what you want.

This is what Marla wants.

"It's too early to fall asleep!" I say. "It's morning! We can go to the lake!"

"It's really okay. I don't think it wants to let me out right now."

"You can't stay in the closet!" I say. But Eleanor has backed up, and so has Astrid. They aren't yelling for Marla to come out. They aren't pulling on the door.

"Shoot," Eleanor says under her breath.

Astrid wipes at her eyes. She has tears in them. The pretty kind.

"Why aren't you trying to get her out?" I say. "Let's take down the door! Dad has tools and stuff, right? We can take it off the hinges."

"We told you guys not to go in," Eleanor says. She shakes

her head. I am getting sick and tired of Eleanor shaking her head.

"Stop telling me all the ways I've messed up!" I say.

"You did mess up," Eleanor says. "You're eleven. What are you doing keeping secrets from us? You can't ask to be treated like one of us, and then act like . . . some baby playing dress-up." There's zero inflection to her tone, so it feels weird to cry or yell back, when she's so monotone.

I let my mouth open a tiny bit, enough to let the shock slip out, and I blink, blink, blink at her.

"Maybe it will open up after she sleeps," Astrid says. She hiccups back a few tears. She holds Eleanor's shoulder, like that might somehow keep Eleanor's meanness back.

"Who would want to be stuck in that awful place?" I say, but secretly I'm wondering if I could decide to get stuck in my closet, on one of my flower-climbing, purple-sea-swimming, glowing-orb-chasing adventures.

I can't stop thinking of the girl in the palace memory. Laurel, who is like me. Laurel, who is maybe stuck in the closet too. Laurel, who Dad says is dead but Mom says is stuck. Laurel, who loved the closets too much, maybe, like Marla.

We listen to the silence behind the closet door. We sit and listen to the way Marla's not coming back right now.

We watch one another stop trying to open the door. We watch one another giving up.

We try to play cards, but everyone loses.

We play the alphabet game, but I can't think of a name that starts with *P*.

"Your own name," Eleanor says.

"Oh. Yeah," I say. I shrug. The game ends.

Astrid makes half a diorama. Eleanor reads a chapter of a book. I close my eyes and imagine everything working out, but it's hard to think of what that would look like.

Hours pass. Doing nothing makes my sisters tired, and soon Eleanor is snoring, and Astrid is breathing heavily, and all I can hear is the ceiling fan and the sound of my heart beating.

I hope maybe Marla has a star inside the closet with her. Something warm and bright and strength-giving. Something that makes her feel hopeful and UnWorried. Something magical.

thirty-two

It's hard to sleep tonight, with Marla trapped in the closet. I keep thinking I hear her rustling around in there. I keep thinking that we could try some other way to get inside. I've seen criminals use clothes hangers and credit cards to magically unlock all kinds of doors and dead bolts and vaults on TV. So surely we can open a closet door with some combination of household objects.

We didn't do enough, that much I'm sure of.

Dad opens jars with butter sometimes. He'll try a tight lid for a few minutes, elbow bent, mouth all crooked with effort, and then he'll grab a stick of butter and push it into the cracks to loosen it up.

"We should use butter on the door," I say. I am sharing a bed with Astrid, whose legs are splayed like a starfish. Her foot is digging into my shin, and I am huddled into approximately one-sixth of her bed.

"Mmmm," Astrid says. I don't know how she sleeps at a time like this. Eleanor is not sleeping, so she's the one who hears me.

"Butter, Silly?" she says. She has a night-light on next to her bed.

"Maybe the door is stuck like a jar gets stuck," I say.

"It's not like a jar," Eleanor says. "It's not a normal thing. It's not some solvable thing. We can't fix it."

I get up to try again and Astrid wakes up with a groan.

"Please stop doing that," Eleanor says while I rattle the doorknob. I can't hear Marla anymore. There's no snoring. No shuffling. No rustling.

"It might change," I say, because it has to be true. "It has to open eventually. Marla will miss us. She'll want to come back."

"The closet in the sewing room. That's probably where Laurel's stuck. That's why Mom doesn't want us trying to go in. That's why it's always locked and Mom's always in there drinking," Astrid says. For once my sisters reached the same conclusions as me, and now they are saying the worst things in the world, the most unimaginable realities.

In a few hours Dad will wake up, and eventually he will not believe us when we say Marla is at a friend's house. Because eventually he will remember that Marla doesn't really have any friends.

Or he won't remember her at all, I think. I'd almost forgotten what Astrid said before, about the time Eleanor stayed too long in the closet and she started to fade from memory. We have to get Marla out before that happens. Something like a ticking time bomb sets off in my chest, and I whir into panic.

"Maybe we need to tell Mom," Eleanor says. "Maybe she knows how to get Marla out."

"Mom's the reason this is happening," Astrid says, and I've never heard her sound so bitter and mad. I never would have guessed Astrid would be the one to get so angry at Mom. All of Astrid's disappearing into different rooms and humming little tunes to herself during fights and losing herself in dioramas and paintings and her own imagination seemed sweet and Astrid-ish. But I guess she was storing up all this rocky feeling.

"If Mom knew what to do, she'd get her sister out. I don't think Mom even remembers," I say.

"That's probably where she preferred to stay," Astrid says. Something's been set off in her, and she's practically a brand-new person. "Mom was probably mean to her too.

Maybe I'll stay inside my own closet, and there will some-day be a whole house of locked closets with little girls stuck inside, trying to avoid Mom."

Angry Astrid is awful.

"Maybe we should tell Dad; he's the one who's here," I say.

"Do you really think Dad could handle it?" Astrid says. "He's barely holding it together now. And Mom's doing well in Arizona. What if we told her and she got sicker? No. Marla's coming out. I'm positive. I know Marla. She'll come out and we don't have to worry Dad and things won't keep getting worse." Astrid's eyes fill with tears. She believes what she's saying, I think, but only barely.

"We have to do something," I say.

"Have Mom and Dad ever really helped make anything better?" Astrid says. "We're stronger without them right now." Her voice falls apart on the last sentence. Falters on the awful trueness of it. "We can do this. Marla will come out. We're sisters. She wouldn't leave us."

"What if Marla never wants to come back to all this?" I say. I'm gesturing to everything—to the room, to us, to Mom not being here and Dad not knowing what to do. I gesture to the fact that we have a ceiling fan instead of an air conditioner and that we moved to New Hampshire for a mom who's not here anyway. To the way even pancakes seem sad lately. Of course Marla chose a closet full of magic over us.

I wouldn't mind returning the star to the closet, I think, and staying there with it. The star and the closet are the only things that help.

I tell my mind to stop thinking those thoughts. We can't give up.

"There's one more thing we can try," I say.

thirty-three

The three of us end up in Marla's room in the middle of the night, in a straight line, looking at the closet door.

"Marla's closet doesn't work, Silly," Eleanor says. She is trying to sound nice but mostly sounds like she needs about a week to herself and a pile of chocolate-chip pancakes.

I open the closet door. It's pointless to argue when we can go inside and see for ourselves.

"This is the memory closet," I say. Astrid's shaking a little, because she knows I wouldn't bring them here for no reason.

I close the door behind us and the closet shifts immediately this time, like it knows how dire the circumstances are, how desperately I need it to come through for me. We are transported directly to the palace. Chandeliers. Marble floors. Violins.

"Oh," Astrid says. "Oh wow." Her eyes are so big they take up her whole face, pretty much. Eleanor sweats next to her. Her fingers tremble.

"But this closet doesn't work," Eleanor says, not able to give it up.

"Marla got it to work. Wait. Wait for it. This isn't the big thing," I say. Which sounds ridiculous, because of course this is a huge thing. It is a strange, strange day when a closet turning into a palace is not the strangest thing happening.

I don't know why we are suddenly allowed to see Mom's memories, but we are. I guess because we need to.

Maybe I don't hate the New Hampshire house so much anymore. Maybe the New Hampshire house wants to help.

"Oh!" Astrid says. The princesses are entering the room, right on time. Girl after girl. I brace myself for Mom's grand entrance, and I gasp at the right moment, along with Astrid and Eleanor, loving the swish of her gown and the easiness of her smile and the way she is both familiar and a total stranger.

"That's. Oh my God. That's . . . ," Astrid says. She doesn't even try to finish the sentence.

"Did you make this, Silly?" Eleanor says. She is filled with wonder. She is asking me for information. She isn't mad or disappearing or telling me I'm ridiculous.

I try to sound as in control as she seems to think I am. I lower my voice and try to keep it calm. "I told you, it's the memory closet. It shows you the memories you need to see." I take my eyes off Mom for one-half second and point Laurel out to my sisters.

Laurel's looking at Mom's arms. Looking at her wrists.

Not at the bracelets, which sparkle and slide around her wrist for being too loose. Laurel is looking at what's underneath the bracelets. The way I've been looking at Marla's wrists, looking for shadows and shades of strange colors— reds and purples and yellows.

Everything about Mom's wrists looks like Marla's—how small they are. The way she touches them every so often with the fingers of her other hand.

And there they are, just like Marla's, as I knew they would be, even if I didn't actually know anything at all. Bruises. A row of them, purple and yellow and red, circling her wrists like the bracelets, but ugly. So, so ugly and painful and tender, and trying hard to be hidden but not.

Eleanor said that maybe Marla reminded Mom of herself as a kid. I didn't know what that meant, but maybe I do now.

I swallow a small sound of pain, understanding too much, too fast.

I let Astrid and Eleanor watch the rest of the ball. I smile when they gasp at Dad's handsomeness, and I shift and fidget right along with them when Mom and Dad dance so closely and look at each other with so much love that it sort of feels like we shouldn't be there at all.

"She's beautiful," Astrid says as Dad drops her into a dip. Mom throws her head back. Her hair nearly touches the floor.

"She's always been beautiful," Eleanor says. Her arms are crossed over her chest, like that might stop her from really seeing all of this. I get it.

"She was the other kind of beautiful before," Astrid says. "Now she's beautiful in a way that makes me sad. But here she's a different kind of beautiful. Lasting. Happy-making. Like how a painting is beautiful because you know it will be the same every day. Like, the great works of art or whatever. Those ballerina paintings. And Monet, with the lily pads. Isn't she lily-pad beautiful now?"

Astrid may be spacey, but she's so much smarter than the rest of us, it's crazy. I guess I forget that sometimes. I nod like I understand, but I don't really, and not only because I can't quite picture Monet or lily pads, but also because I can't think of Mom as anything but the sad kind of beautiful.

Just scary. Or scared. Maybe I'm not totally sure which.

"But look at her wrists," I say. I am getting tired of the sound of the violins and the pattering of feet and the sweetness in the air that says dessert and wine are coming. I'm ready to go home and save our sister.

"She's hurt," Eleanor says.

"She's hurt like Marla," I say. We've never talked about Marla's bruises. We never talked about that day that I hid in my closet and I heard yelps and Mom apologizing and saw Marla hiding her wrists.

"Like Marla?" Astrid looks at me full-on, for the first time since we entered this closet.

"You know," I say, because I have to believe she does. This cannot be another secret that I kept. This cannot be another way that I let down my sisters.

Astrid shakes her head. Eleanor raises her eyebrows.

"Marla. Has bruises on her wrists. I mean, they're probably gone by now. But they were there. From before Mom left. From when she was mad. I mean, it was an accident, like when Mom found out about Henry, and she sort of, you know, pushed you a little."

"What are you saying, Silly?" Eleanor says. "That Mom hurt Marla?"

I spin.

At first I think it's just my brain spinning. But then I

realize it is all of me: my heart, my muscles twisting themselves up, my stomach, my senses. Everything dizzying itself up.

They didn't know.

"You saw Mom get mad at me about Henry?" Astrid says. Her eyes are shiny, and I don't know if they are sad or a little happy. I don't know anything.

It was all on me, it was my responsibility and I messed it up.

And if Mom is any indication, those bruises never go away. They always matter.

"I thought it was one of those things we knew but didn't say out loud," I say. They don't look mad, my sisters. They look sad.

"We need to get out of this closet," Eleanor says.

"Wait, I have to look at another memory," I say. It's time to know how Laurel died. Or if she died. How she got stuck in the closet. Why Mom feels so helpless and angry and gets so drunk. I can't look away anymore.

thirty-four

I can't stop thinking about this one day. It was back when the New Hampshire house was a summer house and not an all-the-time house. Maybe a year ago. Maybe more. It's getting hard to remember, because I used to mark time by Mom's trips Away, but they started happening so often that I lost track. So I started sort of losing track of time in general.

Mom had been sick a lot. I was downstairs. It was the first time I heard her feet pad back and forth across the floor a million times a day. I pictured her like a ghost wandering from room to room, looking for answers to some question that she maybe hadn't even managed to ask. I couldn't decide whether to go check on her. I wasn't sure what I would say, if

I did check on her, or what exactly I would be checking for.

I eventually snuck upstairs, very carefully, because sometimes loud noises or unexpected noises or really all noises upset Mom.

It turned out Mom was at the top of the stairs, and she was crying. She had a mug next to her, and I remember thinking it smelled too sweet to be coffee and too intense to be juice. It smelled like a steak dinner, but without the steak. I didn't like it.

"Wanna watch TV?" I said, like she wasn't crying, or at least like this wasn't weird.

I guess it wasn't that weird. I'd seen Mom cry before. I'd kind of seen Mom cry a lot.

"I forgot to do something," Mom said. She looked confused and tired. I wanted to go back downstairs so I wouldn't have to look at her anymore. Looking at her was giving me a feeling in my stomach. Weight mixed with sickness. My ribs felt full up but my head emptied out. I was pretty sure I would feel okay again if I could get away from her.

"What'd you forget to do?" I asked. "I'll do it for you. Groceries? Laundry?"

"I do more than *chores*," she spat. It was unexpected, the sudden rise of anger, the way her voice sounded more like breaking glass than anything else. "I'm not just a *mother*. I'm not just a *housewife*. I have other things to do, you know. I know you think all I know how to do is shop and make the beds and fix dinner, but I'm a *person*. A whole person. Not that any of you care."

I couldn't breathe. I thought I'd walk down the street for her and pick up milk, or put together Kraft macaroni and cheese for my sisters so they'd have something on the table when they got home. I thought she would be happy if I vacuumed my room or the hallway or something. I don't know. I guess I thought I could fix something small and it would maybe help fix something big.

"I'm sorry," I whispered. I could barely get the words out. And as soon as I'd apologized, I wanted to take it back. I wanted to tell her she was mean and unfair and all kinds of other things.

She kept on crying.

"I can't believe I forgot," she said. She maybe said it a few times. I was mostly looking at a spot on the carpeted stairs.

But I wonder, now, if she was remembering her sister. Remembering the closets, and remembering that she forgot about the closets. Realizing she didn't know where her sister was, and that she hadn't told her daughters anything about her. Remembering she hadn't saved her.

I don't know, but I wasn't going to do that. I wasn't going to forget. I was going to get Marla out.

thirty-five

Astrid tries the door, but I decide they can't leave, so the door doesn't budge.

I ask the memory closet to show us what happened to Laurel, and brace myself for a mirror-image memory of Marla getting stuck in the closet. Instead the ballroom memory fades and we end up at the lake.

The lake looks about the same as it does now—the water's a little darker, there's no grill, the bench that Eleanor reminded me about isn't under the birch tree—but the birch tree is every bit as tall and thin and sloping as I've always known it.

Young Mom and Young Dad are on the dock. Her legs

are over his, and their noses are touching. They kiss every third moment.

"Oh my God, oh my God," Astrid says. She's still recovering from the ballroom, and it's too much, I think, seeing Mom and Dad on our dock in a whole new memory. My heart's pounding too. I know what's coming before I see it.

Laurel rushes into the lake. She swims out far, farther than we've ever been able to go. Past the dock and the buoys and the sandbar.

Mom doesn't see. She doesn't yell after her or glance in her direction to check on her, like she's always telling us to do with one another. There's no lifeguard. There's not even a lifeguard stand.

Mom and Dad won't stop kissing and batting their eyelashes and making dopey love-faces at each other.

"I love you," Mom says maybe for the first time or the hundredth, it's impossible to tell.

Laurel swims out so far that Mom and Dad can't hear the splashing and the flailing, or don't notice it in their love-bubble, but Eleanor, Astrid, and I can see it.

I don't turn away. The speck in the distance that is Laurel vanishes. She's gone.

"Get us out of here," Eleanor says. She puts her hand on my shoulder, and Astrid wraps her arm around my other shoulder.

"That's enough," Astrid whispers, and she's right, it is. I've seen enough.

We walk away from the lake and find the closet door past the birch tree. We find the closet door and leave it all behind.

—⁓—

We can't leave Marla's room for a good, long minute or two. We can't speak or move or think.

I can't think, at least. Maybe Eleanor and Astrid are managing some thoughts.

I'm weeping. Throat-hurting, dripping-wet weeping. "I made so many mistakes. I thought it was okay, I thought it was okay," I say. "I should have told you about Marla. About her wrists. I knew but I didn't want to know."

I kept too many secrets. I turned away from too many things. I'm going to be sick.

"How did Mom forget everything?" Astrid says. "How could Mom forget her little sister and what happened to her?"

"She thought it was her fault," I say, understanding in some strange way. "She probably used to visit memories of her in the memory closet. After. And then at some point I guess . . . she couldn't anymore. The closets stopped being magical for her."

"But she kept trying to go back into all the closets,"

Astrid says. I think we're all remembering listening late at night to Mom pacing to different doors, each one creaking open in its own distinct way, Mom's louder and louder sighs when she didn't find what she needed inside. Sometimes I'd even wake up to Mom in my room, checking inside my closet. I'd pretend to sleep through it.

It only ever happened on the worst nights with the most wine.

"I have one more thing to show you," I say. I'm ready to let them in on the last secret. I shouldn't have had any to begin with.

<hr />

We go into my room. Eleanor and Astrid keep looking at the door, because really we should be in their room, finding a way to save Marla. But I have to show them what I've been hiding first.

"It's a good thing," I say. "Or I think it's a good thing."

I go to the drawer and open the box. I'm scared that when I open it up it will be a box of nothing, and I'll be even more alone.

The star is there, though. Tucked inside the velvet casing, like I left it. Warm, brilliant, radiating. I lift it up.

"Priscilla?" Astrid says. She leans over the box and lets the light of the little star hit her face.

"Is that a . . . what is that?" Eleanor says.

"A star," I say. Astrid nods and moves closer. She closes her eyes and hums an appreciative sound at the way it feels and looks.

"Like, from the sky?" Eleanor says. Her forehead is wrinkling in confusion. Her whole face, actually, is wrinkling in confusion. She takes a step closer to me and Astrid and the star. She reaches one finger toward the light, but retracts it right away.

"From the sky in the closet," I say. "I sort of stole it. Borrowed it. I borrowed it."

"Drop it!" Eleanor screams, almost. But I don't. I hang on even tighter. I need it, need it, need it.

"It's good," I say. "I swear. It's protective or calming or good luck or something. And anyway, I'm going to put it back. I'm only borrowing it, while Mom's gone and stuff. I needed a little magic of my own, you know? Something special."

"You have a whole closet of special whenever you want it,'" Eleanor says. She reaches for the box, but Astrid clamps it shut and takes it from my hands. As soon as its light and warmth are trapped back in the box, I'm sadder, more scared.

"I needed something out here," I say.

"You were so sweet and small and polite for so long," Eleanor says, like we're at the funeral of my former self.

"Let her keep it," Astrid says. She holds the box with the star inside to her chest, and I wonder if she can feel the heat radiating right through her sweatshirt to her heart. God, I hope so.

I give Eleanor an enthusiastic nod.

"You have to return it eventually," Eleanor says. She sounds unhappy to be budging, but even she isn't sure what is right and what is wrong at this point. Even Eleanor doesn't know the rules.

"I will."

"I don't trust you anymore, I don't think," Eleanor says.

"Well, you're gonna have to try," I say. It's the closest I've come to telling Eleanor how to live her life instead of her telling me.

So I stole a star. Borrowed a star. Because when you are sad, you need a little help, sometimes, getting happy again.

thirty-six

We still don't know how to get Marla out, after all that. I'm scared we'll forget her. I know time is running out, if what Astrid says is true. She'll fade more the more time she's in there.

I don't want the three of us to be wandering from room to room, looking for our sister without knowing we are looking for our sister.

She's one of us. We can't pretend she was never here.

Dad is already starting to forget. He was made for forgetting, I think. He forgets the closet and the palace and the champagne river, I'm sure. He forgets what Mom has done to our family. He forgets where he put his keys. He forgets that he is a prince from a fairy tale.

He never forgets the happily-ever-after fairy tales, though. Those he always, always remembers.

I think when you are from a fairy story, you can only remember the things that are here in the real world. Once Marla is in the closet for more than a whole day, she disappears from his world.

The terrible forgetting starts at lunch. Dad comes home from work to have lunch with his girls and doesn't ask about Marla. He does look confused, at least. He spends a lot of time craning his neck to get a good look at the front door and the stairs and the bathroom.

"Marla's on a walk," I say. "That's why she's not here."

He squints at me.

"Okay," he says carefully. "Okay, good. Walking's good." He gets lost in spreading mayonnaise on white bread, and I elbow Astrid so hard she hiccups.

"Marla might be gone for dinner, too," Astrid tries. Eleanor shakes her head at us.

"Was she going to come over for dinner?" Dad says. The words hurt. I basically grab the sandwich out of his hands when he's done assembling it. I eat it in exactly three bites and rush upstairs to sit outside Astrid's closet. Palm to the door, I whisper for Marla to come out.

I don't want to forget her too.

thirty-seven

Dad doesn't set a place for Marla at dinner. He sits me and him on one side of the table, the twins on the other.

"Marla called and told you she wasn't coming?" I say. I want him to remember. Eleanor slumps in her seat and starts shoveling overcooked peas into her mouth. We spent the entire day doing things to the hinges of Astrid's closet door. We used screwdrivers and hammers and wrenches and even a drill. We used a lighter, thinking maybe we could melt the metal.

It didn't matter. The closet door did not open.

We all know, but don't want to know, that we can't do

anything to fix the situation. Marla has to want to come out, but every day she's in there she's farther away, less and less of the Marla we know.

"Marla," Dad says, thoughtful and strange.

"Yeah. Marla," I say, gesturing to the place where she isn't.

"I don't think I've heard from her," he says. The words come out slow and questioning, like he knows he is supposed to know what I am asking about but actually he doesn't understand at all.

"Don't you think you, um, should?" I say. Astrid and Eleanor are silent. Astrid is peeling the skin off her chicken, and Eleanor has nearly finished eating already.

Dad stares at me. He moves his lips a little, trying to form the right word, the right sentence, but coming up with nothing.

thirty-eight

I read with Dad in the living room before bed, trying to craft the perfect way to tell him he is starting to forget his middle daughter and that he needs to get with it.

It is harder than you'd think, to phrase that right.

He eventually stands up and stretches. "I'm gonna hit the hay, Silly-Billy," he says. His tall frame lumbers toward the staircase, but I can't quite let him go.

"Dad?"

He turns to look at me over his shoulder. But instead his gaze catches on the row of framed photographs he hung on the wall when we moved in. There are four pictures, one of each of his daughters. School photos. The kind with accidentally bad hair and forced smiles and weird backgrounds. But Dad likes every picture of us. Always has.

His eyes linger on each picture, one by one. Mine: pigtails and ugly pink shirt. Eleanor: perfectly parted and combed hair, hint of lip gloss. Astrid: messy bun on top of her head and an enormous green turtleneck sweater. Marla: closed-mouth smile and the top of her gray dress.

Dad tilts his head. He points to the last picture but stops himself from saying anything.

"Marla looks good in that picture, right?" I say. I stand up, like that may somehow help him remember her. I'm tempted to shake him, thinking maybe the memories of his daughter are jammed up somewhere between his toes and his brain and I need to get them out.

"Yes?" he says. "I don't remember putting that one up. Did you do it yourself? You know I asked you to check with me before nailing anything in." He's not taking it down or anything, but my heart drops. He thinks I've hung a photograph of some random friend on the wall.

"You put it up, Dad," I say. My voice is shaking and my eyes are burning and my heart is all kinds of wilted and heavy. But I stand up straight and say it loud, so he doesn't forget.

"Huh," he says, and shrugs before heading up the stairs.

thirty-nine

We leave my star outside Astrid's closet door. I don't want to let it leave my bedroom, but for Marla, to save my sister, I'd do anything, I guess.

I didn't know that about myself.

We stay up all night watching my star and the unmoving closet door. The three of us can't all lie down on Eleanor's twin bed, but we can sit on it and let our heads nod sleepily when we get so tired we need a mini nap. We do not sleep longer than a mini nap. We can't afford it.

The star does throw a tiny splash of warm, orangey light on the door. But over the hours, as the night gets darker and colder and more filled with sounds of crickets chirping and owls hoo-hoo-ing, the little bit of light grows. The warmth grows too. Doubles, triples its reach. Soon the heat is hitting my forearms, my toes, my neck. The light is strong but soft, like it's coming from a huge, powerful candle, and even Astrid stops nodding off.

"What's your star doing?" she says, leaning in to me. I didn't know I was old enough for Astrid to lean against. I didn't know I was old enough to take care of my sisters.

"I don't know. I've never left it out," I say. "Maybe it's saving Marla?"

"I'm telling you, Marla has to save herself," Eleanor says. But she's opening her arms wide so that the star's magical heat can hit her body more easily, so it can rush right to her heart and fill her up.

The star gives off a bit of a shimmer. I hadn't noticed it before. It's a sparkling kind of glow. It reminds me of an eye shadow that Eleanor has been putting on recently when she's sneaking off to see her secret boyfriend.

The room is swimmy and glowy and glittery and foggy and so pretty I almost forget about Marla completely.

Almost.

Until I think I hear the door creak.

"It's happening!" I say. Astrid and Eleanor look at me funny. "The door! You hear it, right?"

They shake their heads.

The door isn't opening.

It was the house creaking, the way the New Hampshire house always creaks.

Around six in the morning the sun starts to rise, and the three of us fall asleep in the warm glow of the star that I thought might solve everything but didn't.

forty

Marla has a letter from Mom in the morning. And a package.

"Oh my God," Astrid says. Dad looks up over his newspaper.

"Oh, yes. I wasn't sure what to do with that one," Dad says. He looks utterly confused. He has no idea who Marla is. But he guesses, quite correctly, that he *should* know who Marla is.

"I'll open it," I say.

I wish Marla were here to open it, and short of that I wish Eleanor were here to be in charge of the situation and decide what to do, but she snuck out sometime while Astrid and I were sleeping in. I don't know how, except that maybe the star gave her extra energy. She left a note. It said she was meeting "him" at the lake for an early morning swim and a bagel but that she'd be back soon. It said she was sorry, she should be a better sister, she should try harder, but that she needed her mind to think about something else for a minute.

I don't know if I'm mad or jealous that she's gone. We should all be in it together, sweating it out with no breaks. But it's easy for me to say that, when I have no one else.

All I have is my sisters and my closet and my star.

"I'm going to head to work," Dad says, a little dreamily. He blushes and looks away from the package and the letter.

"You don't want to see what Mom sent?" Astrid says. She's getting in on my game too, determined to get Dad to pay attention, remember, say Marla's name, miss Marla.

Dad pretends not to hear, but he's redder, so I know he's heard. He leaves.

I open the letter first.

> *My Marla,*
> *I'm so sorry. That isn't enough.*
> *I'm staying in Arizona for as long as they tell me to.*
> *It will be a long time.*

Someday I'll tell you everything. Some of it I don't remember, but I'm trying to. Here's what I do know: you can't escape the very sad things. You can lose them for a little while, but they're fast and they'll eventually catch up. And you have to make room for the very beautiful and magic things. Whether they are hidden in closets or right out in the open, on the sparkly surface of the lake, or in the taste of pancakes and bacon on Sunday mornings.

Love,

Mom

Sometimes a thing makes you happy and sad at the same exact time. Relieved and scared.

The idea of Mom not coming back for a long time gives me all those feelings. Astrid crumples up the letter. Throws it on the ground. Maybe Astrid is only angry, and I guess maybe that's okay too.

"Don't open the package," Astrid says. "I don't want to see anything else."

"She said she doesn't remember everything," I say.

"But I remember everything," Astrid says. "Maybe Marla's right, to leave. Maybe we should all be starting over like Eleanor. Or maybe you're right, bringing things out of the closet so that the real world is less awful. Maybe I'm the only one who is doing this all wrong."

I've never seen this look on Astrid's face. It's all screwed up and flushed. She's uncertain and sad. She's not spacing out, staring into the distance or getting lost in a shoe-box diorama. She's right here, feeling everything.

I hug her. She collapses into me and cries. Sometimes I forget how many feelings we're all, each of us, storing inside. Maybe Astrid stares into the distance because she's trying to leave them all behind.

"I remember everything too," I say. It's something I can give my sisters. Something certain and fierce. The things I've seen, and my promise that I won't lose the memories. We stand like that for a while, with Astrid crying and me rubbing her back and wondering at the sudden way I've become the one doing the comforting instead of the one being comforted and protected. "I'm not looking away anymore," I say.

Astrid pulls back. Her eyes are watery and sad and she needs me. She doesn't have to say it this time. I already know it. And I think I almost deserve it. To be needed.

"Look," I say, when Astrid has calmed down enough. "We have to open the package. Maybe it can help. The last package we got helped me learn about Laurel. Maybe this one will do something."

Astrid nods once and I open it.

Inside, layered in so much bubble wrap you'd think it was fine china, is a painting. Oil, like Marla used to do. Small. Imperfect.

It is a night sky. Navy and gray and a little bit black.

No moon.

But stars. So many stars. Dozens of orange-gold stars.

In a corner, there's Mom's signature, and something else. A few words that are too small for me to read. Astrid makes a *hmm* noise, like they mean something to her, and I'm about to ask, but she turns it over so fast I don't have time, and once we see the back I forget all about the front.

On the back, a note from Mom.

> *If she's already gone, go get her.*
> *Dad won't remember her if she's in there.*
> *Remind her what the world has.*
> *The real world. The one we live in.*
>
> *PS: If all else fails, it's all inside you.*

forty-one

We try to call Mom, but some other patient at the rehab answers, and she doesn't understand what we're saying because it's so noisy in their hallway.

"Gretchen! Gretchen! Our mom Gretchen!" we say over and over again.

"Napkin?" the lady on the other end says. She sounds sleepy and confused. "Kitchen?"

"Gretchen!" I yell.

The lady hangs up.

We call Eleanor and tell her to come home immediately.

"Don't go," a boy says in the background. "Let's get back in the water!" I picture Eleanor shaking her wet head, little droplets flying off her hair. I try very hard not to picture her kissing him good-bye. I don't love the idea of Eleanor kissing.

"You have an idea?" she says.

I launch into a description of the note and the painting Mom sent, but Eleanor stops me before I get very far.

"Okay, okay, I'm coming. Deep breaths, Silly. I'll be there."

"You always have to go," her secret boyfriend pouts in the background, and I think I hate him, regardless of how much she likes him.

"My sisters need me!" she calls out to him, while hanging up on me. She'll be here in, like, two seconds. She's a fast runner.

~~~

We get more fabric from the sewing room.

I can't stop myself from trying the sewing room closet.

After all Mom's warnings, the door isn't even locked.

Inside are photo albums and music boxes and dolls and little-kid paintings. The leftovers from Laurel's childhood. The person she was, the fact that she existed, are all hidden in the closet. I want to know if it's magic too, but I'm too scared to shut the door. I only want my closet.

"We're saving our sister," I say, as we look at the place where forgetting happens.

The three of us stand outside my closet, ready and shaking and stuck between hopeful and hopeless. We have fistfuls of construction-paper stars and glitter and yellow thumbtacks. We have as much black fabric as we could scrounge up. We cut up Mom's black wool coat and my navy-blue fleece robe. We are ready.

Except.

I'm a little scared that I'll somehow get stuck too. I guess it wouldn't be a terrible place to live, in a starlit sky that goes as far as my imagination asks it to. But still. I'd miss breakfasts with Dad and the lake and Marla.

I would really, really miss Marla.

I can't get stuck if I don't want to get stuck. If I want to be out here, the closet can't keep me. But Astrid and Eleanor look scared too.

I'll have to go in first. I'll have to show them it's okay.

I go inside and they follow. We keep the door open as we hang the fabric. Keep the door open while we glue and tape and pin and nail the construction-paper stars to the ceiling, walls, every inch of the closet. We are going to need a lot of stars.

"It's only the sky," I say before closing the door. I know they're frightened, and I am too, but the sky and the stars aren't anything to fear.

The shift happens the moment the door is closed. Fabric turns to sky, paper to stars, and we are inside the most chaotic, crowded night sky you've ever seen. The brightness of the stars almost hurts my eyes. The darkness is huge, too, unstoppable. Usually even in New Hampshire, which has, like, three people in it, I can see some lights when it's dark out. Other houses. Neighbors' bonfires. Headlights. Whatever. There's more than the sky and the stars in the real world.

But in here there is only black and navy meeting up in strange patterns, and stars glinting in even stranger patterns, and me and Eleanor and Astrid taking it all in.

"What do we do?" Astrid says. "Do the stars, like, fall? Are they shooting stars or something?"

"We get them. We pull them out of the sky," I say. I pretend, for my sisters, not to be nervous.

I stand on my tiptoes. They don't hold me very well, and I sort of stumble, trying to keep my balance.

"You've got it," Eleanor says.

I try again. Remember to breathe this time. Tense all my muscles, from my toes to my legs to my stomach and shoulders and everywhere in between. I reach my hands up high above my head and right away feel the warmth of dozens of little stars glowing at me. Some of them have pointy edges and jab my fingers when I wave my hands around trying to get ahold of one.

Astrid joins me. She doesn't simply stand on her toes. She leaps into the air, both hands swinging. An animal-like *oof* comes out of her mouth, and she pulls a pile of stars out of the sky.

"Oh!" I say. It hadn't occurred to me to do anything but pick them out one by one. But as soon as Eleanor sees how easy it is, she jumps too, bending her knees deep and making her own growl of effort as she leaps. Soon it is a shower of stars. Eleanor and Astrid bat them out of the sky, taking down five, ten at a time. I push them into a pile, like glowing rocks, but basically weightless. I want to bury myself in them.

"That must be enough," I say.

"More," Eleanor says. "We should have brought a ladder. Silly? Can you fix it?"

I don't know what she means. I'm smaller than both my sisters. I'm smaller than most people my own age, even. I can't reach. I look at her funny and wonder if she needs a reminder about my tininess.

"Make the room smaller. Do your Silly-thing," Eleanor says.

I'd forgotten again. I'm special.

Maybe not in the shiny-haired, long-legged, super-athletic, pretty, talented way that Eleanor is. And not in the artsy, in-her-own-universe, creating-masterpieces-out-of-wire-hangers-and-cotton-balls way that Astrid is. But in some small way that right now is actually huge.

I get back on my tiptoes. Reach my hands over my head. And wish the stars closer.

The night shrinks to the size I'm picturing in my mind. I pick stars, one by one. It feels wrong to swat at them, to treat them like they are candies or beads that you can scoop into a plastic bag. They require more care than that.

I handle each star with the same gentleness I did my first star. Loving the warmth. Loving the way it helps me breathe more easily. Loving the strange, perfect color.

We don't leave any stars in the sky. By the time we are done, we are gathered around a pile of *glow*.

"Wow," I say.

"Wow," Astrid says.

"Wow," Eleanor says.

"How do we get them out?" Eleanor asks. She has stars in her pockets and her hands. We all do, but there's not enough pockets or hands to fit them all.

"I only had one," I say. Astrid plays with a star in one of her hands. Rolls it between her palms and even sniffs at it. "And I think I'm the only one who can take them out. I think it's part of me being, um, special."

"I bet I know how to get them out," Astrid says.

I don't ask. I don't need to know. Whatever she says, we'll do. Because Astrid is nothing if not strange and wonderful and chock-full of the best kind of impulses, the kind that gives her the ability to make her dioramas to begin with, and bring them to the closet, and explore the world around her without fear.

She shivers, and I'd bet there are goosebumps even on her fingertips, her neck.

Astrid puts a star on her tongue. Swallows. Then another. And another.

Astrid is eating the stars.

forty-two

"Astrid!" Eleanor says, so loudly Astrid almost drops the stars in her hands.

Astrid's mouth is too full of stars to respond. But she's not grimacing or throwing up or changing into a lizard or a potato or anything, so something tells me it's okay.

I put a star in my mouth too. We have a whole galaxy to get through, after all.

It doesn't have a taste, so much as a feeling. It doesn't really have weight or substance, so it's more like swallowing hot air than an actual real *thing*. It's warm inside me, but that's it.

"It's okay," I say to Eleanor.

"I thought we were bringing the stars to Marla," Eleanor says.

"I think we are," I say. I don't even know what I mean. Neither does Astrid. But between the stars I can fit in my pockets and tucked into the tops of my socks and the ones being swallowed so we can carry them out of the closet, we are making some serious headway on the pile. And I guess that's sort of all that matters.

We don't get full from the stars. We don't get much of anything, except warm and ready to get Marla. Eleanor finally swallows one too.

"How'd you come up with this?" she says to Astrid, who is now devouring the things with an even confidence, a kind of determination I haven't seen her have maybe ever.

"This thing Mom said," Astrid says. "At the end of her note. 'It's all inside you,' she said. Like, the night sky and the world and the ability to get Marla. It's *inside us*. Or we can put it inside us. I thought she meant believe in yourself, or whatever. And maybe she meant that too. But it occurred to me that sometimes Mom can be sort of literal. And that we need both things—help from the outside and power from the inside? I don't know. It's stupid."

Eleanor stares at Astrid like she's an alien, which she sort of is, so I get it. I stare too. Because Astrid sees something and makes something else out of it, and I want to know how to do that. How to take a clothespin and make it a birch tree. How to take a shoe box and make it a universe. How to take a letter from Mom and make it a solution. How to take words and stars and fear and swallow them down, make them part of the whole.

I eat three more stars, and then the pile is gone and it's time to save Marla. And hope that Marla wants to be saved.

I let us out. I'm still scared. I'm overwhelmed by the fast swallowing and all the warmth that is now both inside and in my hands, my pockets, slipping into my shoes. But it feels good to turn the knob and get a smile from Eleanor and a hip bump from Astrid.

We are able to hang on to the magic of the stars. We move farther and farther away from the closet, but the stars stay bright. We did it together, with my specialness and Astrid's imagination and Eleanor's solid, steady self. A little bit of magic and a lot of us.

Then we are in front of Astrid's closet and laying down stars I took out in my hands. It's a strange kind of ceremony.

There is only that one crack at the bottom of the door where light can get through, so we line all the stars against that space, in a row.

"Marla?" I say, putting my mouth up to that space. "We're here. We're here waiting for you, and you can come out."

There's a long silence, and we all hold our hands together

like we might be praying but we probably aren't.

"Hi," Marla's tiny voice comes through the door. Breathy, like Astrid's. Tired. Not whiny at all. "I can't come out. The door won't open. And I don't want to anyway."

"Marla!" I say, and Astrid and Eleanor echo me.

"What's that light?" Marla says. She doesn't sound excited. She doesn't sound much of anything.

"Stars," I say, matching her hushed tone.

"I don't need stars," she says. "But they're warm. I can feel them. They're warming it up in here."

"Yeah, it's pretty cold in there, huh?" I say. I look to Eleanor and Astrid. They're saying absolutely nothing. "Bet the warmth, um, feels good?"

"I don't mind the cold," Marla says, but there's a little question at the end of the sentence, like maybe she's not totally sure of herself. "I sort of like the cold, actually. It's refreshing."

But I can see her fingers poking at the tiny crack between her side of the door and ours. Reaching toward the warmth.

"We want you out here with us," I say. I press my hands against the closet door, remembering I have warmth and glowiness inside me, too. Remembering that we have a bit of magic in ourselves. I look at my sisters and nod to the door. They snap to it, finally, and touch their own hands to the door of the closet too.

"Whoa! What's that!?" Marla says. At last her voice has a sprinkle in it of something aside from boredom and giving up.

"It's us," I say. "We're here. All of us. For you. To get you out."

"I'm really okay in here. Actually, it's probably better for everyone if I stay. . . ." Her voice sounds even closer, though. Like her mouth is pressed right against the wood, like her whole body is trying to fit itself through the crack.

"We're not okay with you in there," I say. It's so very true.

"We need you out here," Eleanor says at last.

"There's this tree here," Marla says. "It has gold strawberries on it. I mean, strawberries don't even grow on trees, right? But there they are. They're gold. And delicious. And the skies are sort of purple. And, I don't know, I'm okay in here. I fit in here."

"No," Astrid says now. She presses more of her weight against the door. "You belong with us."

"Hey, Marla?" I say. I notice a tiny nick in the wood on one corner of the door. A little place where the wood is splintering, which is funny, since hours of hammering and punching the wood did nothing to make it crack. "Laurel's not actually in there. You need to know that. Laurel never got caught in a closet. She died a long, long time ago, like we were told. She died in the lake, actually. We saw it in your closet. You don't have to be stuck. You're stuck because you don't want to be out here. But we're here. And we want you to come out."

Marla doesn't say anything. Her fingers stay at the bottom of the door, reaching, reaching toward the stars.

forty-three

"Answer us, Marla!" Eleanor screeches.

I pick at the nick in the wood. Another tiny, tiny splinter breaks off. The more I touch the wood, the more it gives in to me.

"Push," I whisper. I don't want Marla to know we can penetrate the door, but I think maybe we can. The combination of her maybe wanting to come out and the three of us being sated with swallowed stars is bringing a new kind of strength.

We push, but the door doesn't budge. I pick at the little splintered part, and another speck flies off.

"Laurel's in here with me," Marla says. "Protecting me.

Like a mom." She whispers the word *mom*. If I really think about it, we've all been whispering the word *mom* for a while now. Like it's a swear or something.

"She's . . . You've seen her?" I say. Eleanor is sweating, drops of it rolling from her forehead to her chin, from her shoulder to her wrist, I assume from her hip down to her ankle, too.

"I can feel her in here with me," Marla says. I pick some more at the door. If I were to take down the entire door at this splinter-by-splinter pace, Marla would be, like, eighty by the time I got her out. I poke Astrid to get her to try too. Quietly, of course.

"Whatever you feel in there isn't real. Isn't Laurel," Eleanor says. "Laurel was a real little girl. She looked like Silly. And she drowned in the lake. Mom only thought she was in the closet sometimes because she was too sad to admit the truth. You only feel Laurel's presence because the closet's giving you what you want. It's not real."

"She's right," I say, because Marla trusts me most of all, and I know that now.

"But what you really need is to be out here with us," Eleanor says. I stand up, and we all three hold hands.

"We have to take what we absolutely need from the closet, and leave the rest," Astrid says. I think of the stars and know that we need to learn how to be strong without them too, but sometimes the magic is needed. Sometimes things hurt so much you have to turn outside yourself for a lift. "We need each other," she says.

Marla's quiet.

"Hey, Marla?" Astrid says. A little glow is coming off her. Like the stars have been digested, and now she's emanating their extra-glowy warm energy. I look to Eleanor, and she's on the golden side too. The room is so warm from all the stars on the floor that it's hard to tell, but I think our temperatures are rising. I think the surface of my skin has changed. I don't get the feeling that it will last. "We're here now," Astrid says. "You don't have to be scared. Or lost. Or whatever. You don't have to be anything. You can be Marla."

"I'm a princess in here," Marla says, but she doesn't sound the way I'd imagine a princess sounding. She doesn't sound that excited about it. "I can be anything in here. Like Mom was. You showed them Mom?"

"I showed them Mom," I say.

"She was happier in the closet."

And maybe I don't totally disagree. She looked so, so happy in the memories in the closet. So pretty and free and in love. In the real world, I've never seen her look like that. I move my mouth around, trying to find words to say.

Eleanor is doing the same, both of us opening and closing our mouths like fish. We're all trying to figure out if maybe Marla and Mom had it right, and we should all stay trapped on the other side.

But.

But.

In spite of everything, Mom's sadness and sickness and the tragedy of her sister and everything else that's gone wrong, she chose our world. She didn't choose the closet. She let it go.

Her problem wasn't leaving the closet, it was working so hard to forget real life.

I catch sight of the window in my peripheral vision. The blinds are open for once, like Eleanor or Astrid needed to remember how pretty pine trees and blue sky are. Outside that window is a sunset. We have spent the whole day visiting closets and gathering stars and waiting for Marla to come back to us, and now the day is changing back into night again. And at first, that's all I think, when I see the splash of pink and blue and yellow and orange and purple outside the window. But then I see how incredible it is that all those colors are marking the sky.

The real sky.

The sky in the real world.

It is a watercolor. It is magical and strange. I guess I

thought it was amazing that I could make the sky pink in my closet, forgetting that the real sky can make itself pink any day it wants.

And it's just as magical, when it's in the real world.

I want to say all this to Marla, and so much more. That the closet is not nearly as magical as the way the sunset is an entirely different color every night. The closet is not as magical as the fact that some days a sunrise is heartbreakingly beautiful and other days it is just light coming into darkness and isn't worth the five-thirty wake-up call at all. The closet is not as magical as the unpredictability of the lake's temperature or the strength of the ocean's waves, or how many blooms will appear in the garden from one year to the next.

Even a dandelion poking up in the middle of a field of green grass is beautiful, when you stop to notice it.

Plus, there are pancakes and bacon, like Mom said. And crickets chirping. And wacky weather patterns. And people who make you laugh even after you've been mad at them for days, and pennies dropped in the middle of the woods, and so many books, and the bite of popcorn with the most butter on it, and Astrid wearing her hair in French braids, and Eleanor's knees when they are freckled from the sun, and Marla's inability to pronounce the words *February* and *restaurant* and *bureau*, and Dad's terrible jokes and the smell of a shampooed head and hours-long games of Monopoly and even, sometimes, Mom laughing or singing along with pop songs we didn't think she'd ever heard of.

I can't say all of that. I put both hands on my throat, like I might need to protect my heart from leaping right out of there.

"I bet you can't even guess what color the sky is here tonight," I say instead. "Your sky in there is always purple, which is pretty, but out here . . . Can you guess?"

"Blue," Marla says, certain. So, so sure. And I would have been too, if she'd been the one asking me. "Blue or black, I guess, if it's late enough."

"Nope. Not blue tonight. Pink," I say. "And orange. And tomorrow it might be gray. Or pure white. Or nearly purple. It's impossible to say."

I know I'm glowing now. I can feel it, and I'm not sure if it's from eating all those stars, or from remembering everything that I *don't* hate, everything that *isn't* the worst, but there it is. A glow. A warmth. A star, inside me, like Astrid said.

I pick a little more at the splinters. They are coming off faster now, this corner of the door coming to pieces, but it won't be enough, if she doesn't want it.

"Pink," Marla says.

"We forgot what was out here. We all forgot," I say.

Eleanor nods, which of course Marla can't see, so I elbow her to make her say it out loud.

"I'm scared of how sad Mom is," Marla says. I almost make her repeat it, that's how small and blue and quiet the words are. But we all pause, and I think there's some delay that helps us hear the words, and we know not to make her say them again, because they are the saddest, scariest, worst words.

"Mom's who reminded me of all the nice little things in the real world," I say. "Mom's remembering. She wrote you a letter. She sent you a package. She wanted you to remember how nice it can be out here."

I dig at the weak parts of the door.

Astrid and Eleanor do too.

And on the other edge of the door, on the far, dark side of the closet, Marla digs too.

forty-four

The sound of Marla's fingers digging into the wood on the other side of the closet makes my heart race.

"The warmth feels good," she says. I don't want to question what's made her change her mind, and that's as good a reason as any.

That, and finally saying the truth.

"We're all scared of how sad Mom is," Astrid says. She matches Marla's low, shy tone, and Eleanor and I dig more, hoping Marla can feel the glow of agreement and safety and general okayness.

She does.

The door comes to pieces.

Marla is there, on the other side, looking like she always does, but different because we missed her and we know now just how much it means to be sisters.

"I thought Mom forgot all about her lost sister in the closet. I didn't know she could never come back, that she had died. I thought she was another person Mom didn't love enough. That she didn't care enough to save her," Marla says.

I know, from the shake in her fingers and her huge, oversize *gulp* after she says it, that she was waiting for herself to turn into a whisper, a voice without a body too. She was waiting to be forgotten.

But we didn't forget her. We couldn't.

And that's the thing she hadn't expected. That's what Marla didn't count on.

That we would always, always remember her.

forty-five

"Eat these," Astrid says, when Marla is on the carpet and we have our backs to the closet, in case looking at it funny will somehow make it pull us back in. She points to the stars, and Marla shivers.

"That seems dangerous," Marla says. But Astrid is sure, *sure* that they are safe. And I am too. We are our normal colors again, tan for Eleanor, the palest pale for Astrid, half sunburnt for me. Whatever the stars did to us was temporary, and Marla, with her shaking and lip biting and skinniness, needs a little temporary boost. Before we say good-bye to the closets forever.

"Don't eat this one, though," I say, and take my star out

of the pile. I put it back in my pocket.

"Silly," Eleanor says, and I almost correct her, because I have certainly earned the name Priscilla today, but somehow it doesn't feel so bad right now, to have a funny, cute, ridiculous nickname that no one else has. "You can't keep that."

"I'm not going to. I promise," I say. Eleanor wants to ask one million follow-up questions, but Astrid gives her a look that says *no* and Marla starts eating the stars and smiling, and we tell her Mom is staying Away for a long, long time, until she's better and then even longer still, and that we are going to save a few stars for Dad to eat so that he gets a little bit of himself back too.

"Mike's mom is going to help," Eleanor says. "I'm going to tell her everything, and she's going to make sure we're okay. She's going to get Dad help too. She works for a place that helps parents be better parents. We won't have secrets like Mom does, okay? We won't have secrets from each other."

"Who's Mike?" I say, even though I know the answer. I grin, because Eleanor said no more secrets, and she can't break her promise so quickly.

"My boyfriend, okay?" she says, blushing.

I like that she's going to let us be part of the little bit of normalcy she's found with him, and I realize that I can call LilyLee's parents and tell them what's happening, and that they'll help too. That we aren't so stuck and alone in New Hampshire. The tallness of the trees and the winding roads of the mountains make it seem like we're far away from everyone else, but we're not.

"It won't be perfect," Astrid says, all wise and breathy and sure. "Some days are going to be the worst. And some days won't be the worst."

"And some will even be great," Marla says.

I love that Marla is the one who says it. Because it makes it even more true.

forty-six

I'm sure I'll tell them later what I've done. They're my sisters, after all, and I can tell them pretty much everything now.

We've made sure Dad remembers Marla, and we slipped some stars into his hamburger, and he gave us big hugs before bed and promised to make pancakes in the morning even though it's not Sunday. He apologized too. For forgetting to sometimes go to the lake with us and for not enforcing bedtime, and for talking too much about Mom when we sort of want to talk about ourselves sometimes.

He talks to Mike's mom. He talks to LilyLee's mom. And I finally, finally talk to LilyLee. She says she and her mom are coming next weekend to check on us. She says she tried writing me postcards and tried calling me but got too sad, from all the missing.

I still feel a little bit of hurt, but I know that sometimes when something hurts, people do whatever they can to make it not hurt. And that sometimes the things people do make it worse.

So I try to be okay with the hurting, and know that it will all be better when we see each other.

"Oh man," Dad says, when we sit on the porch after dinner and drink hot chocolate. "It's going to be all right, you know? And gosh, I love the porch at night."

"Do you think Mom has a porch, where she is?" Marla asks. Dad looks confused, thinking he wasn't supposed to bring up Mom at all, when really we have only ever wanted both. To talk about her and to not talk about her.

"I think Mom has everything she needs," Dad says. I think he's right, and that the pretty night sky she painted for us was her view from a very nice porch, and that when she gets back someday—in many, many months, Dad says— she'll sit on this porch with us and like it. Love it. Think it's beautiful.

And if she isn't able to do that, that will be okay too. Because we will enjoy it ourselves.

When everyone's asleep, I sneak downstairs. We're all so tired, me included, but I have one more thing to do.

It's black, the sky. Not dark blue, not dark gray, full-on for real black. Pricked with stars.

I know I'm not in the closet, and in the real world, I'm not tall enough to reach the sky. But I have a feeling, this once, that the world will surprise me.

I stand on my tiptoes. I get the star from my pocket and reach my hands high into the air. I suck in my stomach and stop breathing and use every bit of concentration I have to focus on getting taller, reaching more. My legs ache, my armpits feel a pull, and I close my eyes.

I let go of the star.

I put it back in the sky.

I come down to my heels and lower my arms before opening my eyes.

It felt like I was sky-high. It felt like I reached high enough to put that star where it belongs.

And I swear, when I look up, squinting at the patterns the stars make all over the sky, complicated patterns Dad promised to teach me one day, I swear I can see my star glinting in the sky, before it fades into the rest of the chaos.

A tiny bit of magic, right here in the real world.

Acknowledgments

All books are collaborations, but this one feels especially like a shared accomplishment with my amazing editor, Anica Rissi. I can't thank you enough for taking time with this story and helping me find my way. To say I couldn't have done it without you would be a massive understatement.

Thank you as well to my wonderful agent, Victoria Marini, who I depend on for so many things, including wisdom and steadiness and generosity and openness. Knowing you loved Silly like I did made writing this possible.

A very special thank-you to Susan Van Metre and Caron Levin. I created the character of Silly and found the seeds of the book in your class, because of the prompts you gave us. What an enormous gift those fifteen minutes of writing every week were. I'm so grateful I wrote outside my comfortable little box and found something new in your class.

Thank you as always to my mom and dad for making sure I loved books and for always supporting my crazy dreams. And thank you to Andy, Jenn, Ellie, and Amy for supporting me from across the ocean.

Thank you to Amy Ewing, Jess Verdi, Caela Carter, Alyson Gerber, Alison Cherry, Lindsay Ribar, Rachele Alpine, and Chelsey Flood for reading Silly's story, challenging me, and sharing in my excitement.

Thank you to wonderful librarian Ally Watkins for taking the time to recommend all kinds of books to me that helped me figure out how to write this book.

Thank you to the incredible group of people who do the magic of making a book an Actual Book: Katherine Tegen, Alexandra Arnold, Alana Whitman, Rosanne Romanello, Valerie Shea, Bethany Reis, Amy Ryan, Heather Daugherty, Barb Fitzsimmons, and so many other wondrous people on the Katherine Tegen Books team.

A special thank-you to Julie McLaughlin for her gorgeous cover illustration. There's nothing like seeing something so beautiful associated with my words.

Thank you to my friends who have been another kind

of family to me. For the times you've listened, for the times you've saved me, for the times you've made me laugh, for the times you've inspired me, for the times you've made me grateful, for the times I've known you're there: Julia Furlan, Anna Bridgforth, Honora Javier, Pallavi Yetur, Mike Mraz, Mark Souza, Brandy Colbert, Kristen Kittscher, Mandy Adams Wolf, Janet Zarecor, Taylor Shann, Meghan Shann, Kea Gilbert, Tracey Roiff, Leigh Poulos, Lindsay Frost, Lizzie Moran, Paul Bausch, and Mary Thompson.

Thank you for your continued love and support: the Spokes Family, the Ross Family, the Haydu Family, the Scallon/Dougherty Family.

And thank you to Frank Scallon. You make writing, and about a million other things, possible.